The Water's
EDGE

ANNE SCHRAFF

SADDLEBACK
EDUCATIONAL PUBLISHING

URBAN UNDERGROUND

SADDLEBACK
EDUCATIONAL PUBLISHING
www.sdlback.com

ISBN-13: 978-1-61651-589-8
ISBN-10: 1-61651-589-9
eBook: 978-1-61247-235-5

Printed in Guangzhou, China
0411/04-56-11

16 15 14 13 12   1 2 3 4 5

CHAPTER ONE

Mama," eight-year-old Katalina Sandoval said at breakfast, "can I have an extra brownie in my lunch today?"

Maria Sandoval, her mother, replied. "Sure, honey. But maybe I should pack you another sandwich if you're hungry."

"No, Mama, it's not for me," Katalina explained. "It's for Andrea Lopez. Yesterday she was crying all during lunch. If she's crying today too, I thought giving her a brownie would make her feel better. You make such good brownies, Mama. They always make me happy, even when I'm sad."

Sixteen-year-old Ernesto Sandoval was Katalina's older brother. He was also a junior at Cesar Chavez High School. Ernesto looked at his little sister. He was proud of her for having such a big heart. But he was worried too.

Luis Sandoval was Katalina's and Ernesto's father. He taught history at Chavez High. He said, "Do you think she was crying because she was hungry? A lot of families are going through hard times right now. They're struggling and sometimes the kids have to go without."

Six-year-old Juanita Sandoval nodded. "I *always* cry when I'm hungry, like when dinner is late."

The Sandovals had three children and another on the way. Ernesto really admired his father. Not only did he teach history in an exciting and interesting way. He also reached out to the kids, especially those in trouble. Ernesto's father had brought several dropouts back to school. He was trying to rescue more who were aimless in the *barrio*.

"No," Katalina answered, as she put butter and raspberry jam on her slice of toast. "I think Andrea is crying 'cause her mama is sick and Andrea feels bad."

"Oh, that's too bad!" Mom said. "Is the doctor giving her medicine so she gets better?"

Katalina looked very sad. She took a small bite of her toast. When she answered, her voice quivered a little. "Andrea's mother has been sick a long time. They didn't have money for a doctor 'cause Andrea's daddy's out of work. Now Andrea's mother is really, *really* sick . . ."

"Sweetheart," Mom said, "what did you say Andrea's last name was?"

"Lopez," Katalina responded.

Ernesto looked at his parents. "That's Cruz Lopez's family," he said. "My friend, Paul Morales, is close to them. Paul and Abel and I took some groceries over there to them. The fridge was empty except for a half jug of milk. Nothing but salt and flour in the cupboards. But Carmen's dad, Councilman Ibarra, he got the family on SNAP."

"What's SNAP?" Katalina chimed in.

"It's a government program that helps people get good food," Ernesto explained. Then, turning to the others, he went on. "Mr. Ibarra also helped them get their health insurance back. When Mr. Lopez got laid off, his boss told him he had no more health coverage. But Mr. Ibarra found out that's a lie. The coverage continues for six months after a layoff. Mr. Lopez has been off work just three months. So now Mrs. Lopez can finally go see a doctor."

Andrea Lopez was in third grade with Katalina at Adams Street Elementary School. The girls were good friends. Katalina always noticed that Andrea didn't have clothes as nice as Katalina's. That made her feel sorry. So once Katalina gave Andrea one of her sweaters. She told Katalina she didn't like it anymore herself, though that was not true.

Ernesto finished his breakfast. He called Paul Morales on his cell phone before heading for school. "Hey Paul," he said. "My little sister, Kat, she goes to school with Cruz's sister, Andrea. She's telling us this morning that Mrs. Lopez is really sick. I thought that problem with the health insurance was cleared up. She was getting some help . . ."

Cruz Lopez and Paul Morales were as close as brothers. One time Cruz, Paul, and their friend Beto Ortiz were hiking in the Anza-Borrego Desert. A rattlesnake bit Paul when they were miles from help. Cruz and Beto carried Paul to the highway, where the paramedics picked him up and saved his life. Ernesto knew Paul would do anything he could for Cruz.

Paul's voice was heavy when he answered. "Mrs. Lopez has been sick a long time. She kept hopin' she'd get better. She pushed off getting the MRI. Mr. Lopez's boss always discouraged employees from getting too many medical procedures. He said it was running up his premiums. Now that she had the insurance card, she went in. They did the exams, and the doctor said it's kinda too late."

Ernesto's heart sank. "What do you mean man?" he asked, even though he knew the answer.

"It's gone too far, Ernie," Paul explained. "When they had insurance, the boss told them not to use it too much. Then he lied and said they had no insurance at all when Mr. Lopez got laid off. Now they're saying it's inoperable, but they're gonna try chemo and radiation."

"Paul, that's terrible," Ernesto gasped. Ernesto's own family was never rich. On his father's teaching salary, they would probably never be. But they always had good health insurance from Dad's job. The family could always go in for checkups and preventative care. The thought of Mom or Dad or the Sandoval kids being sick and unable to afford medical help shocked Ernesto. It seemed inhuman. "Paul," he said, "that shouldn't happen."

"Yeah, right," Paul responded in a bitter voice. "Ernie, will you put your dad on?"

"Sure," Ernesto replied, handing the cell phone to his father. "Paul wants to talk to you, Dad."

"Hello Paul," Luis Sandoval said. "Yes, I'll be at the community college tonight. I'll go there right after I leave Chavez High and meet with my friend in the admissions office. It'll take no more than an hour for us to have the paperwork ready. Cruz and Beto should come by, say, six. We'll have all the papers ready for the guys. Paul, you tell those boys they're doing the smartest thing they've ever done."

Paul said something at the other end of the call. "Yeah, Paul, I know," Dad responded. "It's heartbreaking. But I know that nothing would console Beatrice Lopez more than knowing her boy is taking a solid step toward a good future. She doesn't need any more stress right now. Cruz hanging around the streets and getting into trouble isn't doing her any good. . . . Yeah Paul, you bet."

When Luis Sandoval disconnected the call, he turned to his family. "That was about Cruz and his buddy, Beto. They're getting into the electrician program we've got at the community college while they get their GED. It's a two-year program, and it's going to be hard. But scholarship money is available from the Nicolo Sena fund that Councilman Ibarra just revived. Both Cruz and Beto are eligible for help. Any needy kid in the *barrio* can get help. I've already filled out papers for them."

Maria Sandoval sat sipping her coffee. She had been hungry this morning. Now, as they said, she was eating for two. She was expecting her baby soon. She had felt like another having piece of toast, but suddenly her appetite was gone. She'd seen Beatrice Lopez at a few of the parent's nights at Adams Elementary. She was a frail-looking woman. Ernesto's mother always felt sorry for her because she was so poorly dressed. Obviously, the husband had a menial job, and they had three children. Maria Sandoval remembered

chatting with her about their children. They swapped notes about Katalina, Juanita, and her Andrea and Sarah. Sarah was in the fifth grade. It was just small talk.

Now, looking back, Ernesto's mother wondered whether she could have done something. She wished she'd gotten more friendly with Mrs. Lopez. Perhaps Maria could have helped her with her medical issues. But the Lopez girls seemed happy, and Mrs. Lopez appeared to be all right. There did not seem to be an emergency. Even if there was, Maria Sandoval thought some government agency would be helping.

But apparently nobody was helping.

Maria Sandoval packed an extra brownie in a lunch bag for Andrea.

"Thanks Mama!" Katalina said. "Andrea will feel much better today if she has one of your brownies. You make the best brownies in the whole world. Andrea told me her mama always made cookies for her and her sister. But she doesn't anymore. That's what Andrea said anyway."

Maria Sandoval gave Katalina a special hug. Then she got ready to drive her daughters to school.

After breakfast that morning, Ernesto Sandoval got ready to head out for school. Usually, Ernesto drove his Volvo to school, especially when he was picking up his girlfriend, Naomi Martinez. She lived on Bluebird Street. But lately Naomi had started driving her classic Chevy to school. She'd just bought the car for eighteen hundred dollars, and it was beautiful. The car made Ernesto's Volvo look geeky. Ernesto missed not taking Naomi to school. Although it was a short drive, every minute he could spend with her was a treasure to him. He loved her more than he thought it was possible to love a girl.

Today, Ernesto decided to jog to Chavez High. His best friend, Abel Ruiz, was also jogging down the same street. They lived close to each other. Ernesto and his family lived on Wren Street. The Ruiz family lived near Chavez High too. As Ernesto jogged down Washington Street, he caught up with Abel. They were both good runners, though Ernesto was on the track team, and Abel wasn't.

Ernesto recalled how he'd met Able. Ernesto had been born in the *barrio*. But when he was a small child, his father got a teaching job in Los Angeles. For ten years, the family lived up there. Last year, Luis Sandoval was offered a teaching job at Cesar Chavez High, and the family returned to the *barrio*. In the beginning, Ernesto had felt like a stranger coming to Chavez High. The first student to reach out to him was Abel Ruiz. Ever since then, they had become fast friends. Abel was also very close to Paul Morales. He and Paul had worked at Elena's Donut Shop for a while.

"Abel," Ernesto said, "I found out something today that made me feel awful. Beatrice Lopez, Cruz's mother, she's in a real bad way. Andrea Lopez, Cruz's little sister, is in fourth grade at Adams with Katalina. My sister told us that Andrea cries in school 'cause her mom is so sick."

"Yeah," Abel nodded. "Mr. Lopez's boss is always tryin' to cut corners. When Cruz's mom started bein' sick last year, she didn't want to get checked out. The boss down at the construction company said his premiums go up when employees run up medical bills. So she ignored some really bad symptoms. Then, when she finally had to go in . . . ," Abel shook his head sadly.

"Oh man!" Ernesto groaned. "They got those two little girls. The only good thing is that my dad is helping Cruz get into trade school at the college. Cruz and Beto are filling out the applications tonight."

"That's good," Abel affirmed. "That's somethin'. Poor Mr. Lopez has a sick wife and two little girls. He doesn't need to watch Cruz acting like a gang wannabe. It's bad enough to quit school before he graduated. I'm glad somethin' is being done to help them."

As they approached Chavez High, Ernesto saw his old enemy, Clay Aguirre. Clay had once dated Naomi Martinez, and he had treated her badly. One day, he became very angry with Naomi, and he punched her in the face. Naomi dropped Clay. Eventually Ernesto got close to Naomi, and they fell in love. As Clay saw things, Ernesto had taken his girlfriend away. Clay had never forgiven Ernesto for doing that.

"Hey, big shot!" Clay yelled as Ernesto came on campus. "So you got elected to senior class president for next year. Maybe you'd like for us to curtsy as you go by. Or maybe we could throw flower petals in your path as you walk."

"Knock it off, Aguirre," Ernesto snapped. "I got no time for your stupidity this morning. When we're seniors, I intend to work my rear end off for all the kids. It's not some great big honor. It's a big responsibility, an obligation. That's how I see it."

"Oh man!" Clay Aguirre laughed. "Listen to the dude. He's so good, it's unbelievable. Anybody else elected senior class president would have a big head, but not Sandoval. He's gonna be the servant of the people."

Mira Nuñez, Clay's girlfriend, stood next to him in silence. Clay Aguirre had done everything he could to get Mira elected. He even launched a whispering campaign against Ernesto. Clay had said that Ernesto had been convicted of a DUI and he'd been on drugs in Los Angeles. But the smear campaign didn't work. The students voted overwhelmingly for Ernesto.

"Come on, Clay," Mira urged, unsmilingly. "Let's go to class. The election is over. We shouldn't be standing here yelling insults. Everybody's looking at you."

Ernesto was surprised that Mira was getting some backbone. Usually she went along with whatever Clay was doing like a good little puppy dog. Maybe, Ernesto thought, Mira was finally seeing through Clay. Maybe she'd have the courage to drop him, as Naomi had. Clay Aguirre was an egotistical bully. He didn't know how to treat girls. He was rude to his girlfriends, calling them "stupid" and "dummy."

Most importantly, as far as Ernesto was concerned, he had done the unspeakable by punching Naomi. Every time Ernesto recalled seeing that lovely face disfigured by a bruising from Clay's fist, he wanted to go over and punch the guy into the next county.

Mira moved Clay away. Ernesto walked on, looking for Naomi. Usually she was here by this time. He glanced into the parking lot, looking for her gold Chevy. She'd earned enough money at the yogurt shop—Chill Out—where she worked to afford her own car. It was her dream car. When Ernesto noticed her car arriving, he walked into the parking lot and waited for her.

"Hey babe," Ernesto commented when Naomi got out of the car. "You don't look happy. What's up?"

"Oh," she sighed, "things at home are in turmoil again. Zack dropped out of the community college. He and Dad went at it about that for half the night."

Zack Martinez was Naomi's youngest brother. He was the meek son, willing to do whatever his father asked. Years ago, the two older brothers, Orlando and Manny, had had a bitter fight with their father, Felix Martinez. They had not talked to their father for those years, nor did they even visit the house. But Naomi had worked out a reconciliation, and now the family was healed. Orlando and Manuel were musicians with the Oscar Perez Latin Band in Los Angeles, but now they visited home frequently. Everything was good again in the Martinez family.

Until now.

Wimpy, compliant Zack was the son Felix Martinez always called his "good son" when the older boys were estranged. Now, Zack was doing something against his father's will. It seemed unreal. Eighteen now, Zack had graduated from Chavez High and gone to the community college, though halfheartedly. He wanted to get into the construction business, like his father. Felix Martinez operated large cranes and made good money that appealed to Zack.

But his father would not hear of it. Felix Martinez swore that his son, Zack, would have a better life than he had. He wanted Zack to get an AA degree and then go on to state college for a BA. Felix Martinez said that he had a bad back and that he worked too hard all his life. Now he felt old before his time. He didn't want Zack to wind up that way.

"I can't believe Zack would drop school," Ernesto remarked.

"Well," Naomi explained, "you know Zack has been wanting to dump college for a long time. But he didn't have the guts to tell Dad. So it turns out he's not even been going to classes. Now he's got like a D average. Only reason Dad found out is that Zack's English teacher called the house. She said if Zack didn't turn in his work he was going to get an F. Dad took the call, and he went ballistic."

"Oh boy!" Ernesto groaned. "It must be tough for your father to have his 'good' son rebel like that."

"Yeah," Naomi said. "It's awful. Dad won't let Zack use the pickup. He's saying Zack is busted. He won't let him out of the house. Zack is eighteen years old, Ernie. And Dad is coming down on him like he's a kid. It's awful. Dad's saying Zack is grounded. Grounded! Like a sixth grader. Zack is sitting there in the house, smoldering like a volcano. I don't know what's gonna happen. It's creepy and scary."

"Oh man, poor Zack," Ernesto sympathized.

"You know, Zack has this crummy friend, Steve, at the community college," Naomi said. "You ran into him once, remember? He got Zack in trouble once before, getting him drunk, remember? Zack's trying to call Steve, but Dad's confiscated his cell phone too. It's so unreal. Dad's calling Orlando and Manny up in LA. Dad wants them to come down. Then the three of them—Dad, Orlando, and Manny—are supposed to bully poor Zack into going back to school."

CHAPTER ONE

"I suppose your mom is curled up in some dark corner, just hoping it all goes away," Ernesto remarked. Linda Martinez was a very weak woman. In her world, her husband's word was law. She had no right to voice an opinion about anything. Felix Martinez was nicer to her lately since Orlando and Manny had reconciled with the family. But she was still subservient to her husband.

"Mom is sitting in the backyard," Naomi answered. "She's sitting with Brutus and looking at those elves Dad made in the garden back there. She's pathetic, Ernie."

"You know what, Naomi?" Ernesto commented. "Zack really hates college that much? He wants no part of those history and English classes? I say he should go to some technical school, like Cruz Lopez and Beto are doing. He could get to be a skilled plumber, or electrician, or something. He has the right to be in charge of his own life."

Naomi's beautiful violet eyes grew very large. "You know that, Ernie, and I know that. But Dad is dead set against Zack working with his hands like he's done all his life. Zack is the beloved youngest son, the one who has always stuck by his father. He's the golden boy. I can hear Dad now."

Naomi put on her "mean dad's voice," which always tickled Ernesto. "'My boy,'" Naomi said, mimicking her father, "'ain' gonna be some lousy, stinkin' blue collar stiff.' Oh Ernie, Dad wants Zack to get a liberal arts education. He wants to see Zack sitting behind a big walnut desk in some ritzy office, wearing a suit and tie. Dad is great at his job. He's probably the best big crane operator in the city, and he's well respected. Sometimes they'll bring young guys around to watch him work. But Dad has no respect for his own work. He's got this big dream for Zack—for my brother—but it's a nightmare."

Naomi shook her head sadly. "The tension is so bad in our house it's like something is getting ready to explode."

Naomi and Ernesto continued to walk to class.

Naomi said, "You know what I'm most afraid of, Ernie? I'm scared one morning we'll wake up, and Zack will be gone. He'll just take off. He's just not going to take his father treating him like a bad little middle schooler."

Naomi's voice was shaky. "Oh Ernie, it was so awful for those years that my two older brothers weren't in touch Dad. Those times you sneaked me and Mom down to some little restaurant so we could at least see Orlando and Manny. We'd be shaking in our boots that Dad would find out! Then when we all got together. I was so happy when our family was healed."

Naomi shook her head, as if to say "no" to what could happen. "I don't want to lose Zack. I don't want the whole rotten thing to start over again. And with Zack it'd be even worse. He's not as strong as Orlando and Manny. Zack would start drinking and hanging out with bad people. He'd . . ."

"Babe, just take it easy," Ernesto calmed her. "Let me see if I can think of something. Sometimes I can get through to your dad."

Naomi reached over and put her arm around Ernesto's waist. "Oh Ernie," she sighed, "here I am adding to your problems again. I don't know why you put up with me and my crazy family."

"Babe, I love you so much I'd stick by you if your family was only vampires and werewolves," Ernesto chuckled. "I'd still want to be with you, even if your cousins were biting people in the neck and your uncles were howling at the moon."

That got a laugh from Naomi and Ernesto was glad. He had been able to wipe the frown from her face, even if it was only for the moment.

CHAPTER TWO

When Ernesto got home from school that day, he heard more noise than usual coming from the living room. Usually *Abuela*, Katalina, and Juanita were playing games. But now there was a huge jigsaw puzzle on the floor. *Abuela* was sitting in a nearby chair while four, not two, girls worked on the puzzle.

"Ernie!" Katalina called to him. "This is my friend Andrea and her sister Sarah. They came home with us today. We're all working on this panda puzzle."

Ernesto stood there, looking at the Lopez girls. Andrea was a cute third grader with big, bright eyes. Ernesto had seen her briefly the day that he, Paul, and Abel had brought groceries to the Lopez house. "Hi Andrea," Ernesto said.

Then he saw the older girl, Sarah. She had long dark hair caught up in braids. She was a little older than Andrea. "Hi Sarah," Ernesto said. Ernesto felt a lump in his throat when he thought that perhaps soon these little girls would lose their mother.

Ernesto sat down on the floor with the four girls. "Hey, look." he pointed. "You got a lot of the edges done already. That's cool."

Juanita piped up. "*Abuela* said we have to get the outer pieces in first. 'Cause then it's easier to do the middle. The outside pieces have flat sides."

"I'm terrible at jigsaw puzzles," Ernesto remarked. "They drive me crazy."

Katalina giggled. "I'm good at them, huh, *Abuela*? I can sorta see where the pieces go even when they're sorta the same color."

"Look!" Andrea cried, getting into the spirit of the puzzle. "I found a panda eye!"

Even Sarah got into the puzzle after a few minutes. Ernesto was glad the Lopez girls were absorbed in something . . . at least for a little while.

Later in the afternoon, Mom appeared with strawberry smoothies. All four girls had one, and then Mom took Andrea and Sarah home. When she returned to the Sandoval house, she explained why the Lopez girls had visited. "I thought it would be good if we could have some play dates with Andrea and Sarah. It would help with . . . you know . . . what they're going through."

"That was good, Mom," Ernesto told his mother. Whenever he thought about Beatrice Lopez, he felt terribly sad. He hoped against hope that the chemo and radiation would work.

Ernesto drove his Volvo to work that night at the pizzeria. The pizza shop was owned by Bashar. His brother, Amir, had been shot in the head at his job at the twenty-four-seven store. Bashar had been helping his brother's family while Amir was in the hospital and then recovering at home. Ernesto had been doing double shifts.

Now everything was back to normal, and Ernesto was glad to be back at his three days a week.

"Amir's doing good, huh, Bashar?" Ernesto asked his boss during a lull in business.

"Yeah, he's healing good," Bashar was glad to say. "And pretty soon he's back in school and working at the twenty-four-seven store. He's getting tired of sitting around. He's a very bad patient. He's driving his wife crazy." Bashar laughed hard.

As Ernesto worked, he thought about his father at the community college. About now he would be signing up Cruz Lopez and Beto Ortiz for classes. Paul Morales had been nagging his two friends to get some kind of training for a long time. Ernesto thought they were doing something now because of Cruz's mother.

Mrs. Lopez had pleaded with her son to get some education so that he could make his way in the world. She had worried about Cruz ever since he dropped out of Chavez

High. He was running with bad companions. She lived in fear that one day the police would come to the door and take him away for a serious crime. Now that she was so ill, Cruz could not refuse his mother's plea. And Beto always followed Cruz's lead.

Ernesto went off duty at nine thirty. He decided to drive to the Martinez house on Bluebird to talk with Zack. Maybe, he thought, Naomi would be home from the Ibarras' place. They could all have some coffee and talk. Or maybe just Zack would be there. Ernesto might convince him to stick it out in college for a while. That way, his father could get used to the idea that he had to quit.

Ernesto pulled up in front of the Martinez house. The garage door was open. Both Felix Martinez's pickup and Naomi's gold car were not there. The old family Toyota had been sold. It looked as though nobody was home.

That was odd. Tonight, Naomi hadn't worked at Chill Out, the frozen yogurt shop. She had gone over to the Ibarra house to make Paul Morales feel more comfortable. Paul was visiting his girlfriend, Carmen Ibarra. Whenever he was at the Ibarra house, Carmen's father, Emilio Ibarra, glared at him with less than affection. Mr. Ibarra wished his daughter had a different boyfriend. He didn't like Paul's homie friends like Cruz Lopez and Beto Ortiz. Nor did he like the rattlesnake tattooed on the back of Paul's hand. Ernesto had been invited too, but he had to work. But Naomi should have been back by this time.

Ernesto went to the door anyway. He figured Zack might be sitting inside, feeling awful. Maybe he could cheer him up. He rang the bell.

Ernesto heard Brutus barking. Within a minute, Zack stood in the open doorway. He looked dirty and unkempt. Ernesto smelled beer on his breath.

"Yeah? Waddya want?" Zack asked Ernesto in a very unfriendly voice. Ernesto got along fine with Zack when he was sober.

But, like his father, liquor turned Zack mean. Zack seemed to be in a very dark mood.

"Naomi isn't home yet, huh?" Ernesto asked. He knew she wasn't. But he had to say something.

"You don' see her, do ya?" Zack growled. He started to close the door in Ernesto's face.

Ernesto stuck his foot in the door, blocking it. "Your parents gone too, huh?" he asked. Zack's withering look burned into Ernesto's eyes.

"Nobody home but me. Okay?" Zack snapped.

"Zack," Ernesto said softly, "I know you're going through a hard time. Can I help you in some way?"

"Get lost!" Zack snarled. He tried to close the door again in Ernesto's face. But Ernesto's foot still blocked it.

Ernesto nudged his way into the house. Brutus jumped up on him in a joyous greeting. Ernesto scratched Brutus's head behind his ears. Brutus always liked that.

"Waddya want?" Zack demanded in a sullen voice.

"Zack, I thought maybe we could talk about your problem," Ernesto offered.

"My problem?" Zack almost yelled. "*My problem?* I don't need you comin' here and talkin' like some big shot helpin' me out. You're sixteen years old. I'm eighteen. I'm a man. I don't need a kid to help me. I don't need a punk kid lecturing me."

Ernesto was feeling as though he'd picked a bad time to say something. But he went on anyway.

"Zack," Ernesto responded, "I didn't come here to lecture you. I agree with you. You shouldn't have to go back to college if you don't want to. I was just thinking maybe you should just finish the semester. Then—"

"Man," Zack interrupted, "I've flunked everything. I lied to the old man for weeks. I went every day like I was going to school. But I just hung out with my friends. I can't go back. I don' wanna go back. I don' give a rat's tail about why Washington crossed the Delaware. I don' care about that dude Hannibal or his elephants or the Alps or whatever. I don' care about old fools like Shakespeare or Fitzgerald or Hemingway. They're all just boring writers."

Zack walked over to the cupboard and took out a bottle of whiskey. He poured a shot and swigged it. Then he sipped beer from a can. "That's all garbage to me," Zack ranted. "I wanna get my hands dirty in a real job. I wanna do a man's work."

"Zack, you've had enough of that," Ernesto remarked. "You're already buzzed."

"Mind your own business," Zack snapped. "I can drink if I want to. Dad drinks. He always drank liquor. What's wrong with me drinkin'? I'm a man. I can drink if I wanna. I can do anythin' I want."

"Zack," Ernesto tried again, "maybe you could go back to the community college. But you could take courses in construction or plumbing. You know those two guys who hang with my friend, Paul

Morales? Cruz and Beto. They're learning to be electricians at the community college and—"

Zack slammed the beer can on the end table. A splash of beer spurted from the can and on the table. "I never want to see that stinking college again as long as I live," he snarled. "You better go home now, Sandoval. I got nothin' to say to you. And you got nothin' to say that I want to hear. You're a suck-up, Sandoval. Everybody knows that."

Zack took a gulp of beer. "I tried to be like that," he continued. "I did everything my father tol' me to do. I did that for a long time. No more. I'm a man now. I'm a Martinez. We don't take nothin' offa nobody. So just get outta here. I'm expectin' somebody, okay?"

The room lit up from a car's headlights as it came into the driveway. Ernesto thought Naomi or her parents were coming home. But it was a strange car, a banged-up Honda. Steve got out of the car. Steve was Zack's old drinking buddy from college. He seemed unsteady on his feet. The front door was open, and he walked in. Steve looked at Ernesto and remembered him. Several months ago, Ernesto had seen Steve and Zack both drunk and trying to drive. Ernesto drove Steve off and bullied Zack into letting him drive the pickup home.

"Waddya doing here?" Steve demanded of Ernesto.

"He's just leavin', Steve," Zack declared.

"What's going down around here?" Ernesto asked. He began to see the picture, and it wasn't good. These two drunken young men were about to hit the road.

"Me and Zack are getting outta here, man," Steve said. "So don't give us no trouble. Okay?"

"You're both too drunk to drive," Ernesto told them.

"Here we go again," Steve groaned. "Listen dude, you're not pulling that on us again. Get outta our way, man. I swear I'll bust your skull. Just get outta my way."

Ernesto pulled out his cell phone. "I'm tipping the cops that two drunks in a Honda are coming down Bluebird Street," he warned them.

Steve lunged at Ernesto. He swung his hand and knocked the cell phone from Ernesto's hand. The phone flew across the room. It crashed against the fireplace mantel and broke into pieces.

Brutus barked nervously, sensing the hostility. He growled at Steve, but Brutus wasn't a fighter. His tail went between his legs, and he got behind the sofa. He kept growling softly from there.

Steve threw a fast punch at Ernesto, knocking him off his feet. Ernesto hadn't expected such violence—or so quickly. Ernesto was on the floor for a second. Then he scrambled to his feet, but Steve was like a madman. He had fire in his eyes. He had Ernesto outweighed by about fifty pounds. He was big and mean, and he was used to brawling.

"I'm not letting you go out there drunk," Ernesto shouted, dodging a punch by Steve. "You could get killed or kill some innocent people." Zack stood back, looking stunned. Steve came at Ernesto again, but Ernesto deflected still another blow. Still, Ernesto had to step back. He tripped on the coffee table and fell backward. His head struck an end table. Ernesto was woozy for a second or two. He felt blood trickling from his head down his cheek. The room was a blur for a few seconds.

Then things happened at a hundred miles an hour. Steve and Zack beat it out the front door. In a moment, the Honda was screeching out of the driveway. Ernesto could hear the engine growl as the car whipped around and took off on Bluebird. Nobody was left in the house but Ernesto and Brutus. Brutus came out from behind the couch and sniffed Ernesto's head sympathetically. The confused dog whined forlornly, aware that something was very wrong.

Ernesto was still a little wobbly. But he found another cell phone lying on the sofa and dialed the police. He told them two drunks were driving a dark blue Honda. He said they'd just left Bluebird and were going west on Tremayne. That's the best he could do. He hadn't gotten the Honda's license number.

Ernesto sat on the sofa with Brutus at his feet. The dog looked up at him from time to time with soulful eyes.

A few minutes later, Naomi's car pulled into the garage. As she came in the front door, she remarked, "Ernie, I saw your car parked out there at the curb and—" The she saw the dried blood on his cheek and gasped, "You're bleeding! Oh my God! What happened?" Naomi rushed to the sofa and sat down beside Ernesto.

"I'm okay," Ernesto assured her. "I just hit my head. It bled a lot at first. Probably just a nick."

Ernesto started telling Naomi what had happened. "I came by to talk to Zack. I thought I could help." He glanced at Naomi with a look that said, "Duh!" He shrugged his shoulders and went on. "Zack was kinda drunk. Then Steve showed up. They planned to go off together. Steve was mean drunk. I tried to stop them from driving because they were both way over the limit. I tried to stop them. But Steve smashed my cell phone, and then he decked me. He caught me off balance, and my head hit the end table over there. Not a good night, babe."

"Oh Ernie!" Naomi groaned. She gently parted Ernesto's hair with her fingertips. She made sure the wound was not serious. It was a surface cut. It looked bad only because it bled a lot. "Oh Ernie," she suggested, "let me put a little hydrogen peroxide on it."

"Okay," Ernesto agreed. Within a few minutes, Naomi had swabbed on the hydrogen peroxide. It foamed a little but helped to clean up the blood. She then cleaned the blood away from his scalp and face with tissues.

"Oh Ernie," she said over and over, "I'm sorry. I'm so sorry. Do you want to go to Urgent Care? I'll drive you right away." Urgent Care was a privately owned clinic in town.

"No, no, it's okay. I'm fine," Ernesto insisted. "That guy Steve, he's big. And he's tough. He caught me off guard. He really packs a punch. But if I hadn't hit that end table, maybe I could have stopped them. They're out there now, driving drunk. I called the police, and told them what the car looks like. I didn't have the license number. But maybe the cops can head them off anyway. I hope they get stopped before they have an accident."

Naomi put her arm around Ernesto's shoulders. "I'm so sorry, babe. This is just awful. You were trying to do a good thing and—"

"Where are your parents, Naomi?" Ernesto asked abruptly.

"Oh," Naomi responded, "they went to this little farewell get-together for Monte Esposito. This is his last night as a free man. They wanted to give him a send-off."

Felix Martinez's cousin, Monte Esposito, lost his city council seat to Emilio Ibarra. Then Esposito was indicted on bribery charges. He did a plea bargain that required him to serve six months in jail. He'd been given some time to make personal arrangements. But now he had to report to prison in the morning.

It didn't surprise Ernesto that Mr. Martinez wanted to be with his cousin tonight. The two men were very close. It just about broke Felix Martinez's heart when Monte lost his job in the city council. It broke more when Monte admitted to Felix that he had been bribed and had to go to jail. Still, tonight was a very bad night for Mr. Martinez to leave his angry, distraught son alone.

"Naomi," Ernesto said, getting up and heading for the door. "I feel much better now. When your parents get home, tell them what happened. But please don't make it worse than it was. Be sure to tell them that I'm fine. Steve busted my cell phone. That doesn't make me very happy. If I ever run into the guy again, I plan to take it out of his hide. But other than that, I'm okay."

"Okay, Ernie," Naomi agreed, still looking deeply sad. "Poor baby. I just feel so bad."

"Naomi," Ernesto continued, "tell your father that I let the police know about them driving around. If they're busted, you may have to get Zack out of jail. Zack had been drinking beer. I smelled it on his breath. Then he started in on the whiskey from the cupboard over there. Steve was really bombed. He looked like he'd been drinking all day. If he's driving, he's a menace."

Ernesto turned to go but wheeled back to face Naomi. "Oh, one more thing. You've got to get it through to your father that Zack can't be grounded like a kid. The guy is bitter and angry. He's like a ticking time bomb. Your father has got to back off when Zack comes home."

"*If* he comes home," Naomi commented.

Before he left, Naomi gave Ernesto a long hug and a kiss. "Should I follow you home in my car to make sure you make it all right, babe?" she asked.

"Babe," Ernesto replied with a faint smile. "I live on Wren Street, remember? It's one street over from here. I can make it. I had worse bumps and cuts when I used to ride my skateboard."

Naomi kissed him one more time, on the lips. Then she let him go.

Ernesto was more angry than anything else. He was sucker punched. He never expected that kind of violence. He wished he could meet Steve again. Next time, he'd be ready. Next time, Steve would be on the deck.

Ernesto drove home slowly. He wasn't angry at Zack. Ernesto knew where the guy was coming from. He had to break away of Mr. Martinez's grip.

CHAPTER THREE

Ernesto hurried quickly into his house without anyone seeing him. He went to the bathroom and washed his hair. The small swelling had already gone down. He put hydrogen peroxide on the wound. Just then Katalina came up behind him and asked, "Is that blood in the sink, Ernie?" She peered into the basin before Ernesto could run more water. "Oooooo, it *is* blood!" she exclaimed.

"Kat, stop spying on me. I'm just washing my hair," Ernesto told her. He grabbed a towel and started drying his thick blue-black mop of hair.

Maria Sandoval came down the hall. "What's this about blood?" she demanded.

"Oh man," Ernesto groaned. "A guy can't get away with anything around here." He turned and looked at his mother. He tried to change the subject. "I guess Dad's still at the college, huh?"

"Don't change the subject," Mom commanded. "How did you get hurt?"

"Oh, I stopped over at the Martinez house and—" Ernesto began.

"I bet Mr. Martinez hit you over the head," Katalina piped up. "He's pretty mean sometimes. Mama said he's worse than Brutus."

"No, no," Ernesto objected. "I just fell and hit my head on an end table."

Mom noticed the pieces of Ernesto's cell phone lying on the sink. "And the cell phone flew from your hands as you were falling, right?" Mom asked in a skeptical voice.

"Yeah," Ernesto said. "Something like that."

"Ernesto Sandoval," Mom ordered in a strident voice, "this is your mother talking to you. In about one minute I am going to call the Martinez house to find out what happened. Answer me!"

"Okay Mom," Ernesto responded, "okay. I went over to the Martinez house to talk to Zack. They've been having problems with Zack. I thought maybe I could help. He's quit school and stuff."

"That wimp of a boy is giving them trouble?" Mom asked scornfully.

"Yeah," Ernesto replied. "Alcohol can turn a wimp into a monster sometimes. Felix Martinez got really angry with Zack when he quit school. He grounded Zack. Took away his cell phone, won't let him use the truck. Insists he stay in his room and sit in the corner like a five-year-old."

"Don't be sarcastic, Ernie," Mom chided.

"Well, anyway," Ernie continued. "Fool that I am, I was trying to talk Zack into being a good boy and returning to college. I figured he might just end the semester to placate old Dad. Then in comes Zack's buddy, Steve. He's a mean drunk if there ever was one."

Ernesto tossed the bloody towel into the hamper and brushed his hair. "So they're both drunk. Really drunk. And they're gonna drive around in Steve's car. I try to stop them. And Steve decks me. My cell phone gets smashed. Steve takes another swing at me. I duck it but lose my balance. As I go down, I hit my head on the corner of the table. While I'm woozy on the floor, the two drunks take off."

"That is an outrage," Mom stormed. "You should have called the police. Those boys should be charged with aggravated assault!"

"Mom," Ernesto said soothingly, "I did call the police. I told them about the Honda going down Tremayne with a drunk at the wheel. That's as far as I want to go. I don't want to put Zack in jail, okay? Or the other jerk. It was just a drunken brawl. Unfortunately, the only sober one in the room— idiot me—gets decked."

Ernesto silently vowed to get back at Steve. "Anyway," he went on, "I hope the cops stopped the Honda and both jerks got busted. The thing is, Felix Martinez came down too hard on Zack. The guy's eighteen. He's an adult. You don't tell an adult that he's gotta go to college or else he's grounded. Zack'll have a major hangover tomorrow. He'll come crawling back to his father, all apologetic. Once he's sober, Zack will be Daddy's contrite little boy again."

"Well, I wish you'd call the police and pressed charges for assault," Mom fumed. Mom knew she could press charges as the parent of a minor. But she knew Ernesto better. She chose to go with his wishes.

"Oh boy!" Ernesto groaned. The small wound on his head had finally stopped bleeding. He went into the kitchen to get something to eat.

Ernesto made himself a peanut butter and jelly sandwich. He was eating it when the home phone rang.

"Ernie," Felix Martinez screamed into the phone. "That dirty, rotten, lousy punk kid of mine attacked you!"

"Oh man!" Ernesto sighed softly, closing his eyes. He had once assured Naomi that he would always love her. He would love her even if she came from a family of vampires and werewolves. Now he thought perhaps she did.

"Mr. Martinez," Ernesto explained. "I'm fine. I'm good. Zack didn't attack me. He's with that creep Steve. He threw the punch. Zack's pretty buzzed. Steve's drunk too. They're driving around out there."

Then Ernesto decided to have his say. "Mr. Martinez, I'm not the one to give you advice, I know. But Zack's pretty bent about being grounded. Maybe he just needs a little room. He'll to come around in his own time."

Mr. Martinez had calmed down a little. He didn't respond to Ernesto's comment about Zack. "You sure you're okay, Ernie?" he asked.

"I'm fine," Ernesto assured him.

"Ernie," Mr. Martinez told him, "we're all sorry over here. We're really sorry. You're such a great kid, Ernie. Tryin' to do the right thing. But we'll make it up to you, boy. We'll make sure you get a new cell phone. Naomi said those punks busted yours."

They spoke another minute or so and then ended the call. And Ernesto was glad the call was over.

Luis Sandoval came home just after ten fifteen, "Oh, you still up, Ernie?" he asked. He saw his son working on the computer in his room.

"Yeah, Dad. How did it go with Cruz and Beto. Did they get signed up okay?" Ernesto asked.

"Yes, they did," Ernesto's father answered. "They scared me, though. They were supposed to show up at six. I waited and waited, hoping they weren't going to bail on me. Finally, about nine they came in. They gave some lame reason for being late."

Mr. Sandoval took a deep breath and exhaled. "Well, they're signed up anyway. But, you know, Cruz has changed. I know he's worried about his mom, and that's part of it. He's gotten much more serious since Amir was shot at the twenty-four-seven store, and we were wondering if Cruz was involved. Cruz and Beto both promised me they'd work hard on their training classes. Ah! They got it wrong tonight and showed up late. But I believe those boys are firmly on the right track now."

Mom stood in the doorway, her face still grim. "Has Ernie told you he was attacked over at the Martinez house tonight?" she asked.

Dad didn't say anything for a moment. Then he gasped, "*What?*"

"Those barbarians over there," Mom fumed. "The son, Zack, he and his evil friend were violently drunk. Somebody named Steve. Poor Ernie was trying to talk some sense into Zack. That Steve knocked Ernie down and smashed his cell phone.

49

Ernie has a big gash in his head. I told Ernie he should be calling the police. He should have those criminals thrown into jail where they belong. But no."

"A gash in your head, son?" Luis Sandoval cried.

"Just a little nick when my head hit the end table," Ernesto explained. "We put hydrogen peroxide on, and it's okay."

Luis Sandoval came over and gently probed his son's mop of hair for the wound. "I can't find it," he said.

"The 'gash' is sort of gone," Ernesto responded.

"Just the same," Mom insisted, her anger unabated. "There's no excuse for them knocking poor Ernie down and smashing his cell phone. That's unacceptable behavior!"

"They smashed your cell phone?" Dad asked, looking distressed.

"Yeah," Ernesto said. "But Mr. Martinez has already called and said he'd pay for a new one. Right after Zack and Steve took off, I called the police. I told them to be on the lookout for two drunks in a Honda on Tremayne Street."

"Good," Dad commented. But he continued to look bewildered.

"It's not good enough," Mom persisted. "They should be in jail for assault. It's all that Felix Martinez's fault. He's been raging around that house now for years like a Visigoth. No wonder the boy is like that."

"A Visigoth?" Ernesto repeated. He vaguely remembered something about Visigoths from his medieval history. He pictured them as hairy wild men who were always pillaging.

"Yes," Dad explained, for the moment in his teaching mode. "The Visigoths were a Germanic tribe that sacked Rome in 410."

No one said anything for a second or two.

"Well," Mom went on, "it just makes me furious. I was nice enough to invite the Martinez family when the local news covered my book signing. I included them in that. The whole Martinez family was there, including Brutus. Zack was nice as pie with Brutus."

Maria Sandoval had based her picture book, *Thunder and Princess*, on the Martinez's pit bull. She had wanted them to be in the news report with her. "And now to think they attacked you, Ernie."

"*They* didn't attack me, Mom," Ernesto pointed out. "It wasn't like the whole family came at me with pitchforks. It was just Steve and Zack who were drunk and stupid. Mr. Martinez feels terrible. He said he was really sorry."

"And well he should feel terrible," Mom snapped. "It's all his fault. He's such a wild man. Naturally his son has no self-control either." Mom stomped off to take her shower and get ready for bed.

"You know, Dad," Ernesto remarked with a half smile on his face. "I always thought if somebody could kill me, it would have been Clay Aguirre. I never dreamed it would be Naomi's brother."

Dad smiled faintly too. "Your mom is very upset," he replied. "She's a true Mama Bear. When somebody hurts her cub, look out."

"Yeah," Ernesto agreed.

Mr. Sandoval sat down on Ernie's bed, leaned back on his hands, and crossed his legs. "You know, Ernie," Dad said, "It's not easy being a parent. You love your children more than life itself. You want them to have a happy, good life. But then they make choices that you don't necessarily agree with. Your mother and I love Naomi Martinez because she's a wonderful girl. Still, she *is* from *that* family."

Dad checked his son's reaction. He needed see whether he was getting his point across. "I think your mother would rather you weren't dating a Martinez. And, you know, if things progress enough with Naomi, you could have Felix Martinez as your father-in-law for years and years . . ."

"Yeah," Ernesto acknowledged. It didn't matter though. He loved Naomi.

53

"I was talking to poor Emilio Ibarra the other day," Dad continued. "We were talking, as fathers do, about their children. I mean, Emilio loves his little girl, Carmen. Just as your mother and I love you and the girls. Emilio was hoping Carmen would find a nice, solid boy, a normal kid from a family he knew. Instead, she's going with Paul Morales. Poor Emilio. It bothers him that Carmen seems to be falling in love with Paul. He can't get over that rattlesnake tattooed on Paul's hand. And the whole mystery about Paul's family doesn't help either."

"Yeah," was all Ernesto could say. What else could he say?

"Emilio and I," Dad continued, "we had some nice strong coffee. We said, 'Wouldn't it have been nice if Ernie and Carmen had hit it off?' I mean, wouldn't that have been something? Emilio thinks the world of you, Ernie. He first met you at that party, right after we moved back down here from Los Angeles. Correct? Well, he thought you liked Carmen, and she certainly liked you. Poor Emilio was so excited. He thought you'd be the perfect boyfriend for his little girl."

"Yeah," Ernesto responded. "I remember that party. Mr. Ibarra kept looking at me like a robin looks at a worm. He kept following me around. He was asking me questions all night, like he was interviewing me. I was scared he'd demand I get engaged to Carmen then and there. I was really spooked. I was never so glad to get out of a place."

"Just think, though," Dad suggested, looking wistful, "if you and Carmen had hit it off. You'd have lovely girl like Carmen from that great family where everybody is, you know, *normal*. Not that the Martinez family isn't normal, mind you. But Felix is . . . uh . . . different. What a relief that would have been for Emilio. He wouldn't have to deal with the Morales boy with the rattlesnake on his hand. But I guess it wasn't meant to be."

"I guess not," Ernesto responded.

"Well," Dad sighed tiredly, "it's getting late. I believe I'll take a quick shower. I don't hear the water running. So I think your mom is finished."

Mr. Sandoval stood and stretched. "The baby will be here before we know it, Ernie," he said. "And your mom needs a lot of love and support. She, you know, is a bit more excitable than usual these days."

Dad came over to where Ernesto was sitting. He laid a gentle hand on his son's shoulder. "Love you, son," he said. "More than I can say."

"Back at you, Dad," Ernesto replied with a grin.

After Dad left his room, Ernesto used the home phone to call Naomi.

"Everything okay, babe?" he asked.

"It's quieted down now, thank God," she reported. "You sure you're okay, Ernie? Your head doesn't hurt, does it?"

"I feel great," Ernesto assured her. "It's like it didn't even happen."

Of course, he did not mention Mom's calling Naomi's family barbarians and Visigoths. And, of course, he would never tell Naomi about what his father had said. He would never say his Dad would like to see Ernesto and Carmen get together. He'd never admit that his Dad wanted him to date someone from a "normal" family. No mention of any of this would ever pass his lips.

"Haven't heard anything from Zack yet, huh?" was all Ernesto did say.

"No," Naomi replied. "If he and Steve were busted, we probably would have heard by now. Whoever was driving would be in jail."

"Stay tuned, I guess," Ernesto said.

"I'm so sorry. I love you with all my heart. Goodnight, babe," Naomi signed off.

"Love you more," Ernesto told her.

In the morning, before Ernesto left for school, the home phone rang. Dad answered and had a short conversation. Then he hollered down the hallway to Ernesto. It was Paul Morales calling.

"Hey man," Paul said. "Been tryin' to get you on your cell. But I'm not getting' through. Wassup?"

"Long story," Ernesto answered. "Tell you when I see you. In the meantime, I'm using my Dad's cell." Ernesto gave him the number.

"Me and Carmen," Paul explained, "we're gonna dine out at this awesome new restaurant. We'd like you and Naomi to come along. I invited your parents too, when your Dad picked up the phone. But your father said your mom is too close to having her munchkin. But we'd love for you guys to join us. It's on me. This Friday night."

"What's the occasion, Paul?" Ernesto asked.

"Just that you guys have been so great helping out Cruz and his family," Paul responded. "Your dad's getting Cruz and Beto into trade school, getting the scholarships lined up. It's just all you guys've done to help. I just wanted to do it. You're an awesome friend, dude. There's a trait that I share with elephants. I never forget a real friend—or an enemy."

"Great," Ernesto said, "I'll check with Naomi. I'm sure she can make it. It's coming at a good time for Naomi too, Paul. Her brother Zack left college. Now he's out there in the *barrio* somewhere and . . . well, it's part of that long story."

Ernesto called Naomi about the invitation. She said Friday was good for her. She'd heard about the new restaurant too. She was looking forward to checking it out. Ernesto confirmed with Paul.

There was no news about Zack for the next few days. Ernesto thought he'd be home long before now. Ernesto figured Zack was hiding out somewhere, working up enough courage to come home. This was, after all, the only time in his life he had really defied his father. Also, maybe Zack was worrying about what had happened to Ernesto. Maybe he thought he was in trouble over that. Ernesto wished he could get in touch with Zack and let him know it was safe to go home.

Ernesto picked Naomi up on Friday evening. As they drove to the restaurant, she said, "Mom's worried sick about Zack. Dad is more mad than worried. He's on the phone to Orlando all the time. Dad wants him to come down and help him corral Zack. Zack made a couple friends at college, besides Steve. He's probably crashed at one of their apartments near the college."

Naomi was quiet. Ernesto figured she was trying to remember names. "I wish I'd paid more attention when Zack mentioned his friends. I think there was a guy named Pete something. I don't remember a last name. But Zack seemed real close to Pete. He said one time that Pete lived real close to the college."

When they pulled into the parking lot of the restaurant, Naomi pointed, "There's Paul's pickup. He and Carmen are here already."

"I'm glad he's here," Ernesto remarked with a grin. "He's paying for dinner!"

They spotted Paul and Carmen in a leather booth with a view of the bay. You could see the lights twinkling on the boats.

Ernesto and his girl slid in opposite Paul and Carmen. "This is a cool place," Ernesto exclaimed.

"Yeah, it just opened," Carmen replied. "They've got salmon and halibut. But I'm going with the Mexican menu. I'm ordering the catfish tacos."

Ernesto and Naomi looked at the menu. "Mmm," Naomi read the description. "'Lightly fried tacos filled with catfish and pickled red onions.' And they got black beans with them. I'm with you, Carmen."

"Salmon for me," Ernesto decided.

"Ditto dude," Paul Morales agreed.

Soon they were eating their salads and waiting for the entrees.

Paul spoke to Ernesto. "Ernie, you should have heard Cruz raving about how great your dad was down at the college. He and his friend had all the right papers for Cruz and Beto to fill out. They had the scholarship applications approved already. Those dumb dudes would never have taken this big step without your dad's help. I've been nagging them forever to learn enough to earn a decent wage. But I've been talking to a wall. Your father, he has a gift for reaching guys."

"That's great, Paul," Ernesto responded. "Cruz's mom has spent years worrying about her boy. It's got to be a consolation to her now to have him in a program."

"Cruz's mom," Paul declared, "she just lit up when we told her. She didn't even know anything about this Nicolo Sena Scholarship. Mr. Lopez never heard of it. Very few people know about it."

"Yeah," Ernesto agreed. "A councilman who used to handle the *barrio* district years ago started it. He and some local business-people set it up. It was in honor of Nicolo Sena, the first kid from the *barrio* to die in Vietnam. Then Monte Esposito came along. He just let the program die on the vine. Carmen, your dad revived it."

Carmen smiled. "Yeah, Dad's really proud of that. Paul, you know Ernie's father went to college on a Nicolo Sena Scholarship about twenty years ago. That's how he got to be a teacher."

"Well, that was money well spent," Paul asserted. "The guy is sure doing more than teaching history. He's paying back big time by helping guys like Cruz and Beto. Usually Cruz's mom is so weak and listless. She just came alive when we told her how Cruz was finally on the right track."

"How's Mrs. Lopez doing on the chemo and radiation?" Naomi asked.

"They won't know for a week or so," Paul relied. "They'll do a MRI to see if it's done any good."

"What happened to her makes me sick," Naomi remarked. "She needed care a year ago. If she'd gotten it, she'd have a good chance of being well now. Miguel Lopez has worked so hard all his life. I don't think the man has ever had a vacation. He had health benefits even when he got laid off. But his boss told him he didn't. It's so wrong."

Naomi speared a piece of salad with her fork. "My dad was talking about Mr. Lopez last night. Sometimes he's worked with Cruz's dad on construction jobs. He said Mr. Lopez is a nice man, but he lets people intimidate him. My dad has really good health benefits on his job. He insisted on them. He said he'd quit if he didn't like what he saw."

"Mr. Lopez was always talking about your dad, Naomi," Paul remarked with a laugh. "From what I hear, nobody intimidates Felix Martinez. I give the guy credit for that. I know somebody like him must be hard to live with. But he's tough enough to take care of his family. You gotta be tough in this world. You gotta take care of yourself and your family. Nobody else is gonna do it for you."

"Most people don't even understand their insurance benefits," Carmen commented.

"All that fine print. You pay the premiums. When you need help, you find that you've slipped through a loophole."

Paul Morales got a dark look on his face. "That company Mr. Lopez worked for—the one that told him not to go for checkups . . . somebody should throw a nice big chunk of concrete right through their front window some dark night."

"Don't do it, dude!" Ernesto cautioned. "All you'd accomplish is to get yourself busted and ruin your life. The world doesn't have enough good guys, Paul. You're one of them. So don't mess up. We need you, man. We need the good ones."

"Here, here!" Carmen cheered.

"Ernie's mom brought the Lopez girls over to their house for a play date," Naomi remarked. "They had a lot of fun. Ernie told me they worked on a huge jigsaw puzzle."

"That was great," Paul said. "Andrea told me about it. Your sister, Katalina, she's

Andrea's best friend, Ernie. You got a nice mom. I wish somebody like her had adopted me and my brother David. Maybe we'd have turned out more like you, dude."

"You're doing okay, man," Ernesto told him. "Hey, this salmon doesn't taste anything like the stuff you get in cans. This is good stuff."

CHAPTER FOUR

Ernesto didn't plan on telling Paul and Carmen what had happened at the Martinez house. He didn't want to embarrass Naomi. But in the middle of dinner, Naomi asked, "Did Ernie tell you guys what happened at our house? He went over there to try to help Zack."

"No!" Paul answered. "He didn't say anything about that. What happened?"

"Oh!" Naomi exclaimed. "It was ugly. My brother Zack's been going to the community college, and he hates it. Zack wants to go with Dad to the construction jobs and learn a trade. They got an apprentice program where Dad works. Zack wants into that. But Dad's forcing him to stay in school."

Naomi sipped her iced tea. "Anyway, poor Ernie goes over there to talk with Zack. Usually, they got along good. Well, nobody's home but Zack, and he's drunk. My brother's a nice guy, but he shouldn't drink. Beer or booze turns him into a whole other person, and it's not pretty. If that's not bad enough, in comes Zack's horrible friend, Steve. Now Steve is even more drunk and mean than Zack. Then they decide to leave. Mr. Nice—my responsible Ernie—doesn't want the guys driving drunk. So he tries to stop them. And Ernie gets decked, gashes his head, and has his cell phone smashed."

Paul's head swiveled from Naomi to Ernesto. Paul stared at him in shock.

Ernesto spoke first. "That was the long story I told you about on Tuesday."

"Man," Paul gasped, "you got attacked, and you didn't even tell me? You shoulda called me right away. I'd of left them both on their butts."

Ernesto laughed. "There wasn't time. They were out the door before I could get up."

"But dude," Paul asked, "isn't Zack the spineless brother who does everything right? Now he teams up with another drunk and beats you up?"

"I told you, Paul," Naomi explained. "Liquor makes Zack a monster. Now he's out there somewhere in the *barrio*. Mom's wringing her hands and crying. Dad's stomping around the house, cursing him. The whole house is in an uproar again. The only member of the family I can peacefully hang with is Brutus."

"You got any idea where Zack went?" Paul asked.

"I think he's crashed with some guys he knows from college," Naomi guessed. "Orlando and Manny are coming down from Los Angeles tomorrow to hunt for Zack. I'm going with them."

"Hey," Ernesto volunteered, "I'll take you all in the Volvo. I'll join in the search party too."

"Oh Ernie," Naomi protested. "My horrible family has done enough damage to you. I hate to ruin your Saturday."

"Come on," Ernesto said. "For you, babe, I'd do anything."

Naomi smiled at Paul and Carmen. She said, "You guys, you know what Ernie said to me the other day? He said he'd stick with me even if my family was made up of vampires and werewolves. Is he wonderful or what?"

Paul smirked and spoke. "Naomi, I hate to mention this. I've seen your dad when he hasn't shaved in a couple days. And he's yelling about something, and his eyes look sorta red-rimmed. It has crossed my mind that he just might *be* a werewolf."

Naomi punched Paul in the shoulder. He leaned back and laughed. Then, after they finished their dessert, Paul spoke to Ernesto and Naomi. "Good luck with the hunt tomorrow. A kid like Zack, he's been under his father's thumb for most of his life. He could get pretty lost runnin' on his own. I'll ask around with my homies and see if anybody knows anything. If I find out anything, I'll call you guys. Ernie, you still using your dad's cell phone?"

Ernesto nodded yes.

As Naomi and Ernesto walked out of the restaurant with Paul and Carmen, Naomi made an announcement. "Orlando and Manny are doing a little gig with the Oscar Perez band at Hortencia's tomorrow night. Orlando's nagging me to come on stage and do a song. He's even got this real sexy evening gown I could wear."

"Go for it, girl," Paul urged her. "You might find out you like it. Who knows? You might be the next big thing. The next Beyoncé or Rihanna."

"Yeah, right," Naomi protested. "If I do get up and sing some stupid song, that'll be the end of it. Orlando and Manny love that sort of thing. But it's not for me. I'd never want to get into that."

"I don't know," Paul objected. "You're pretty hot, Naomi. Oscar Perez has a great band. But it's missing somethin' not having a girl singer. You might just be the thing to launch Perez into super stardom—and you with him."

"My mom loves to sing and dance," Carmen interjected. "Maybe you'd discover a new side of yourself. It might be a revelation, girl."

"I don't think so," Naomi said.

"We're coming to Hortencia's Saturday night," Carmen asserted. "Right, Paul?"

"Hey," Paul said, laughing, "I wouldn't miss it for the world, seeing this babe strut her stuff."

Naomi and Ernesto said their thank-yous and good-byes. Then they drove out of the parking lot.

As the Volvo turned onto the road home, Naomi spoke. "I remember Zack talking about a class in medieval history. The instructor was named Hawthorne. I think the Pete he mentioned might have been in that class too. It was a Saturday class. I think that jerk Steve was in the class too. That might be a good place to start looking for Zack tomorrow. If we can find out where this Steve lives, we might find Zack sleeping on his sofa. He's got to be holed up with one of the guys from college, either Steve or this Pete guy."

"Good idea," Ernesto agreed. "Naomi, I'll be over to Hortencia's at nine tomorrow morning. I'll pick up Orlando and Manny, then I'll be at your house to pick you up. And we'll be on our way." They stopped for a red light.

"Ernie, you're an angel," Naomi told him, kissing his cheek.

The next morning, Ernesto, Orlando, and Manuel walked into the Martinez house. Felix Martinez was in his favorite easy chair, still fuming. He looked at his two older sons and shook his head. "I can't believe Zack done this to us. And what he done to you, Ernie. I can't believe it. Orlando, Manny, did Ernie tell you what the kid and his rotten friend did to him?"

"No," Orlando replied, looking at Ernesto.

"Orlando," Mr. Martinez said before Ernesto could speak. "Him and this criminal, Steve, they smashed Ernie's cell phone. They knocked him down. And he got a gash on his head. They almost killed him."

"No, no!" Ernesto protested to Orlando and Manny quickly. "It wasn't that big a deal."

"I'm tellin' you guys, all three of you," Felix Martinez stormed. "I'm gonna get my hands on that little punk. He's gonna be the sorriest dude in the *barrio*. I ain't used my belt on any of my kids in a long time, but—"

A strange look came over Orlando's face. Of all the sons, he was the most like his father. He looked like his father had looked as a young man. He had Felix Martinez's temper, and he could carry grudges for a long time. Orlando had decked his own father several years ago. Felix Martinez was abusing his wife, Linda. For all those years, father and son were bitterly estranged.

Neither would budge. Only Naomi's intervention finally brought them back together.

"Dad," Orlando stated coldly, "listen to me and listen good. Me and Manny and Naomi and Ernie are gonna look for Zack. We're gonna bring him home if we can. But not until you promise me you won't lay a violent hand on him. You've been browbeating Zack all his life, Dad. He's eighteen now. He's a man."

Maybe Orlando realized he was coming on too strong. His tone changed a little. He sounded a little more as though he was asking, not demanding. "You're not gonna use your belt on my brother, right? Dad, swear to me right now that it ain't gonna happen. Otherwise, I'm done with this search right now. And so's Manny."

Naomi's mother stood in the doorway, a look of shock on her face. She could hardly believe her son had the courage to talk to his father in such a harsh voice.

Manuel Martinez was a lot less aggressive than Orlando. But he'd also been estranged from the family for three years after a fight with his father. "Orlando's right, Dad," he agreed. "I don't want no part of bringing Zack home for a bad beating."

"They're right, Dad," Naomi chimed in. Her voice was calm but firm. "Zack's a good guy. He just got boxed in, and he didn't know where to turn. What he did— tearing out of here with Steve—was an act of desperation. When he comes home, we've got to talk. No hitting."

Felix Martinez sat there for a few seconds, looking at his three children. He turned to Ernesto and asked a question in a shaky voice. "You against me on this too, Ernie?"

"I'm not against you, Mr. Martinez," Ernesto responded. "But I do think everyone'll all be better off talking than hitting."

"Okay," the man replied in a barely audible voice. "You got my word. I swear— no hitting."

"Good," Orlando said. He put his hand on his father's shoulder and slapped it a few times quickly. Then he turned to his brother, sister, and Ernesto. "Let's go." Orlando glanced at his mother and gave her a smile. "Don't look so sad, Mama. We'll find him and bring him home. And tonight we celebrate. *Carne asada*!"

Ernesto climbed behind the wheel of the car, and Naomi sat beside him. Orlando and Manny got into the back.

"This is nice of you, Ernie," Orlando said.

"No problem," Ernesto replied.

They drove to the community college and found Mr. Hawthorne's medieval history classroom. It was about twenty minutes to class, and many students were milling around. Ernesto spotted a friendly-looking girl and he said, "Hey, excuse me. We're looking for Zack Martinez. He's in this class, right?" Ernesto knew, of course, that Zack would not be coming to class. But he didn't want to admit that.

"Oh," the girl replied. "He's been out of class for a long time. He dropped out or something."

"Is there a guy named Steve in this class too?" Orlando asked.

"Yeah," the girl answered. "He flunked out too."

"You wouldn't know where Steve lives, would you?" Naomi asked.

The girl shook her head. "I didn't know either of the guys, except just to see them in class."

A boy was standing nearby listening. "Hey dudes, you want to get in touch with Zack? You need to talk to Pete Gamboa. He and Zack and Steve are buddies," he told them.

Ernesto looked around. "Pete here?" he asked.

"Not yet," the boy nodded no. "Wait, there he is, in the blue hoodie." He called out, "Hey Pete! These guys're looking for Zack."

Ernesto looked at a short, pudgy dark-skinned boy in the blue hoodie. Pete Gamboa shuffled over to them, his hands stuffed in his jacket. He had a little bit of a gangster walk. He looked hostile.

"I'm Zack's sister," Naomi said to Pete. "These two guys are our brothers. This is Ernie, my friend. We're all worried about Zack. He left home a coupla days ago, and he was kinda buzzed. Our mom's real worried too."

"I'm Orlando Martinez, Zack's oldest brother," Orlando added, extending his hand. Pete Gamboa ignored it.

"We want to take Zack home," Naomi went on. "Do you know where he is?"

Pete Gamboa just stood there staring at her. "Don't know nothin'," was all he said.

Ernesto could tell the boy was lying. Anybody could tell. "Look," Ernesto said, "I don't know what Zack told. But he doesn't have to be afraid to come home. It's cool."

"He said his old man's pretty fierce," Pete Gamboa responded. As he spoke, his head bobbed a little. Then he stared at Ernesto with his head cocked at a slant. "He said his old man would make Big Foot look like a little girl. That's what Zack told me.

Last time I seen him, that is. Long time ago. I don't think he wants to go home . . . wherever he is."

"Look," Orlando offered, "we got it all worked out at home. Zack doesn't have to be afraid."

"Yeah?" Pete Gamboa asked, his head now cocked at Orlando. His look was one of mock sincerity. "Well, I don't know where he is. I think maybe he went up to LA or somethin'. I gotta go to class now. *Adios.*" He turned on his heel and walked into the classroom.

Orlando turned to the others. "Pete's a little cranky. Musta been up all night studying."

Ernesto looked at Orlando. "He knows where Zack is. But this guy Pete, he doesn't believe it's safe for Zack to go home. Zack must be really scared. He knows he's defied his father like he never did before. He's terrified. He's put that on Gamboa, and the guy isn't going to betray him."

"So what do we do now?" Manny asked.

"I saw the car Pete Gamboa got out of," Naomi said. "That white car. I bet if we were really careful, we could follow him home. Pete seems like he really cares about Zack. Like he wants to protect him. I bet Zack's in his pad."

"Okay," Orlando agreed. "Let's go over to the school cafeteria and get something to eat. We'll hang out there until Hawthorne's class is over. Then we'll try to track Pete Gamboa to his place."

"And let's hope it's Pete's last class of the day," Ernesto added.

"And that he's going straight home," Manny added.

"Well, let's also hope we get lucky," Orlando responded.

The four of them sat, eating burritos, for the next hour. From the window of their cafeteria table, they could see the classroom.

"You know," Orlando grumbled. "Dad's really messed up our family by being such a bear. He drove me and Manny out for all that time. He's been harassing Mom. I know the guy loves us. He'd die for any one of us, but he's too tough."

Orlando took a small bite of burrito. He chewed and swallowed it quickly. "I guess he was raised that way. He just carried on like his own old man. I remember our grandfather beating up on his son, Dad's brother, when Uncle Leon was a grown man. Leon turned out as mean as a snake. He wouldn't even forgive his own poor daughter for marrying a guy he didn't like."

Naomi nodded. "I remember being in the hospital when Uncle Leon was dying. Our cousin stood in the corridor, screaming 'Daddy! Daddy!' But he wouldn't forgive her. I was fourteen when that happened. You guys, that's why I worked so hard to get our family back together. I didn't want it to end up that way with us. And now I know Dad's getting better. He's not as mean and hard as he used to be."

"Yeah," Orlando agreed. "He never would have let me talk to him like I did today. You're right, Sis. The old bear has trimmed his claws."

"A little," Manny added.

A few minutes before class was due to end, the four of them walked to Ernesto's Volvo. They all got into the car and waited in the parking lot. Their eyes were glued on Pete Gamboa's white car.

"We'll follow him at a distance," Ernesto suggested. "He doesn't know our car. He probably won't even notice. Lots of cars'll be pulling out at the same time."

"There's a lot of student housing over there," Naomi said, glancing south to some apartment buildings. "One time Zack told me five and six kids sometimes crowd into an apartment where like two are supposed to live."

"Yeah," Ernesto said. "When the landlord comes to check, the extra kids hide or take off."

Pete Gamboa came slowly walking toward his car. A few minutes later, he pulled out of the parking lot. Ernesto followed at a distance. Pete Gamboa turned a corner and headed for the apartment buildings. He pulled to the curb near a green stucco building, got out, and started toward one of the stairs leading up to a unit.

Ernesto pulled the Volvo over to the curb across from the apartment building. He was opening the door when Orlando urged, "Wait! Wait! He looks like he's taking the stairs. We can see from here what door he goes in."

Pete started up the stairs to the second level of apartments. From the car, everyone could see the whole row of doors. Pete unlocked the third green door from the right and went inside. Inside the Volvo, the four figured out their next move.

"We can't rap on the door," Orlando said. "The minute the dude sees one of us, he'll slam the door in our faces."

"Well, we can't just bust in," Ernesto remarked.

Orlando looked at Naomi. "Sis, you look the most innocent of us. What if you just went up those stairs and rapped on that door? Then you put on the sweetest voice you can muster. You plead with the guy to let you see your brother and talk to him."

"Okay," Naomi agreed, "here goes."

"Don't forget to bat those beautiful violet eyes!" Orlando called after her.

Ernesto hoped she wasn't walking into trouble.

CHAPTER FIVE

Naomi walked up the stairs and knocked on the green door. There was no doorbell. In a few seconds, Pete Gamboa opened the door and looked at her. "You're the chick who was with those dudes," he said. "I told you I don' know where Zack is."

"Please," Naomi begged. "I'm so worried about my brother. Our whole family is sick about it. I'm Naomi."

Pete Gamboa spent a few very long seconds staring at the girl. Then he turned and yelled into the apartment. "Zack, some chick's here. Says her name's Naomi. Says she's your sister. Your family's worried about you. Waddya want me to do, man?"

"I'll talk to Naomi," Zack hollered from inside the messy apartment. Slowly Zack came into view. He stood just inside the doorway.

"Naomi," he told her, "he ain't never gonna forgive me. Ernie won't forgive me either. Steve hurt Ernie, Naomi. I'm sorry 'bout that. I'm so scared. I just wish I was dead."

Naomi moved closer to the doorway. She didn't want to scare him away.

"Zack, it's okay," she assured him. "You don't have to worry about anything. Ernie's right downstairs, waiting for us. He's not mad at you. He's fine. He wasn't hurt. Dad's going to buy him a new cell phone. But, Zack, Dad made a promise to us all. There won't be any hitting or anything when you come home. Okay? Mom's making *carne asada* to celebrate you coming home. How does that sound?"

Zack stood there, visibly shaking. "Dad's gonna get the belt and—"

"No, Zack, wrong," Naomi objected. "Believe me. He swore he wouldn't. Orlando and Manny are with us down in the car. They're on your side, Zack."

"I . . . I didn't think Steve would hit Ernie," Zack whimpered. He was near tears. "I know I wasn't bein' friendly with him. But I'd never hurt Ernie."

Naomi stepped forward, close to Zack. She put her arms around him. "I know you wouldn't hit Ernie. I know that, Zack," she soothed him. "Ernie knows that too. Where's Steve now?"

"In jail," Zack told her.

"In jail?" Naomi gasped. "What happened?"

"We had a big fight after we left the house," Zack explained. "I told Steve he shouldna hit Ernie. I thought maybe Ernie was hurt bad. I wanted to turn around and go back to the house. I needed to make sure Ernie was okay. But Steve cussed me out. He threw me out of the car and drove away. I got on a bus and came over here to Pete's place."

Zack pushed back from Naomi. His hands held her arms. He looked directly at her. "I was so scared about Ernie. I called his house to see if he was in the hospital. But I only had Ernie's cell phone number, and it wasn't workin', you know. Later on I heard the cops got Steve for a DUI. I don't know if he's still in jail. Maybe his parents bailed him out. Naomi, you sure Ernie's okay? You're not lyin', are you?"

By this time Ernesto, Orlando, and Manny had made their way up the stairs to the unit's doorway.

The first face Zack saw outside was Ernesto's. A big smile broke out on Zack's face. Zack rushed toward Ernesto, bouncing off the door jamb. "Ernie! You *are* okay! Naomi told me you were okay. But I didn't believe her. Dude, I'm *so* sorry. I never woulda hit you, man. I was sick with fear. I'm telling you, Ernie. I'm done with that creep, Steve. I'm never gonna talk to him again. He called me a weakling. He told me I needed whiskey to be a man, and

I drank too much . . . " Zack's voice trailed off.

Ernesto gave Zack a hug. "It's okay man."

Orlando came in, followed by Manny.

"Zack," Orlando told his brother, "we had a heart-to-heart with old Dad."

Naomi, Ernesto, and Manny all exchanged glances. Their faces said, without words, "Heart-to-heart?"

Orlando continued, "We're gonna have a nice family talk about the future. You're a grown man. You can do what you want. But it's safe to come home, back to the nutsy Martinez clan."

Zack turned and looked at Pete Gamboa. "Pete, man, thanks for letting me hang here."

"Anytime, *amigo*," Pete told him. He threw his hand forward, dipping his shoulder at the same time. They shook, hugged, and slapped each other's back. Suddenly, Pete Gamboa seemed like a pretty nice guy.

Pete stepped back and nodded his head toward the group at the doorway. "You sure you want to go with them, dude?"

"Yeah," Zack replied. He thanked Pete again, and the boys fist-bumped.

Pete stood in the doorway and waved, as Zack went down the stairs. Zack, his family, and Ernesto all piled into the car. It was crowded in the backseat, but the brothers made it work.

As they drove toward the Martinez house, Zack explained himself. "I just couldn't take bein' in school anymore. I just couldn't stand studyin' English and history and that stuff. I hated every minute of it. I wanna get my hands dirty. I wanna smooth a cement slab and learn how to put a roof on a building. I love that kinda thing."

Zack turned to Orlando, who was squished in the backseat with him. "Remember when I was little? A coupla times I went to work with Dad? He wasn't a crane operator then. He was doin' regular construction work. He mixed cement and smoothed slabs.

I thought, 'Yeah, that's what I want.' But Dad kept saying that's just for jerks. I hadda get my BA from State. I hadda sit behind a desk doing what-I-don't-know."

Zack stared straight ahead. "All those years of college just stretched out before me . . . like a prison sentence. I was willin' to finish high school. But then two years in the community college, another two, three years in State . . . " Zack shook his head.

"Yeah, well," Orlando responded, "we're not all scholars."

The Volvo was quiet for the rest of the drive.

The Volvo pulled into the Martinez driveway at two thirty. Linda Martinez and Brutus came flying out the front door. Mom had been watching and praying at the window. She saw the Volvo down the street. As it drew near, she spotted her youngest son in the backseat with his brothers.

"Oh Zack! Oh baby!" Mom cried, embracing Zack when he got out of the car. "I worried so. Oh Zack, I'm so happy to see you! Come on in the house. Tonight we're going to celebrate with *carne asada* and *frijoles negros*! Whatever you want, honey!"

"Mom," Zack asked a little nervously. "Is he—?"

"Your father is all right," Mom assured her son. "He was so worried too. He acted mad. But you know that's how he is. As time went by and you weren't home, he got more and more worried."

The four boys and Naomi came in the front door together. Felix Martinez was standing there. Zack could hardly bear to look at him. Finally, he raised his eyes to his father. "Dad, I'm awful sorry . . . "

Felix Martinez shook his head no. "Boy," he declared, "it's him, that one there, Ernie. He's the one. You should be apologizing to him after what you and that scum Steve did."

"He did already apologize to me, Mr. Martinez," Ernesto explained. "And I accepted it. Steve was the one who busted my cell phone and hit me, not Zack."

"Where's that scum Steve now?" Dad asked.

"In jail," Zack told his dad. "The cops busted him for a DUI. Then he got in a fight with the cops. So they got him for that too."

"That's where he belongs, in the slammer," Felix Martinez declared with satisfaction. "I hope they keep him there for a long time."

"Dad," Zack said in a broken voice. "I'm really, *really* sorry about everything. I know I let you down. But I just wanna go and do what you do, Dad. I wanna build things. I wanna go to the construction site like you do. I wanna get in that apprentice program they got where you work. Dad, that's all I want. I love stuff like that. I see you every morning getting in the cab of your pickup. You got your hard hat on the seat beside you. And I wanna go with you. I wanna . . . you know . . . *be like you, Dad*."

Felix Martinez stood there staring at his son. He had wanted to see his youngest boy wearing a cap and gown and graduating from State. He had wanted Zack to get a job where he'd sit at a polished walnut desk, giving orders. He pictured Zack in a business suit, white shirt, and tie. Zack would jet around the country, meeting with people about some big merger or something. Those images faded slowly from the father's mind. As they did, Felix Martinez felt a little sad.

Then the father walked over, grabbed his son, and gave him a long hug. "I'm glad you're home, boy," he whispered to him. "We'll see about getting you that hard hat."

Ernesto saw that it was time for the family to be by themselves. He turned to leave. But before Ernesto left the Martinez house, Mr. Martinez stopped him. "Just a minute, Ernie." He disappeared for a moment. Then he came back with a bag from the electronics store that Paul Morales managed.

"Here you go, Ernie," Mr. Martinez said as he held the bag out to the boy. "It's a good one. Better than what you had. I went in to talk to that guy, Paul. He said this is 'cool,' whatever that means to you guys."

"Wow, thanks, Mr. Martinez," Ernesto said, taking the new cell phone. "But you shouldn't have had to pay for what Steve did."

Felix Martinez smiled. "Ernie, it's my pleasure. It happened in my house. I am taking responsibility."

That Saturday night, Naomi Martinez appeared at Hortencia's in a dress that shocked Ernesto. She had many beautiful outfits. But this was a glittering evening gown. It looked like the kind you'd see on famous stars as they walked down the red carpet to major events. Naomi looked awesome in the red off-the-shoulder gown.

"Look at her!" Felix Martinez exclaimed, nudging Linda. "The kid is a knockout!"

Naomi stood at the microphone, staring out to a point beyond and above the audience. The spotlight made her gown glitter.

The band played the lead-in to her number. Oscar and Manny Martinez soloed behind her. They played melancholy chords and rhythms that touched the heart. Naomi leaned into the microphone. Then, softly, she began her song about unrequited love and longing.

Paul Morales leaned over to Ernesto. He whispered, half in jest and half seriously, "Dude, you got problems."

"What do you mean?" Ernesto asked. But he knew exactly what Paul was driving at. What if Naomi got a taste of the glitz and glitter? Was she going to be happy with a high schooler from the *barrio*?"

"Oh Paul," Carmen quietly scolded, "that's ridiculous. Naomi isn't buying into this. She's got her feet on the ground."

Ernesto *was* worried. He had never seen Naomi look so amazing. She always looked beautiful. But now she looked like an entirely different person—a beautiful, glamorous stranger. Oscar was staging things just right. Ernesto couldn't get his mind around this new image. Naomi didn't look like the girl who snuggled against him in the Volvo. She wasn't the girl who walked with him at the beach, holding his hand and laughing. She was no longer the girl who ate supersized hamburgers with him and giggled at his lame jokes.

Ernesto looked around at the audience. The guys were drooling. Ernesto felt sick. With the spotlight on Naomi, she shimmered. Her lovely voice caressed the Spanish lyrics. She was mesmerizing. She was hot. Right before Ernesto's eyes, his girl had become a superstar. That's what he thought, anyway.

The last few lyrics were sung, and the last few sad chords were played. The spotlight dimmed until the stage was in darkness. A moment passed. Then the applause was deafening. Naomi had already disappeared into the back. She had said she would do just one number. Then, she'd said, she would change out of her fancy clothes.

Ernesto wondered whether she was done with entertaining. Or would she reappear to sizzle again before her adoring fans?

Would the Naomi Martinez he knew and loved still exist after that performance? Surely all that whistling and cheering had gone to her head. It had to. She had stepped into a new and magical world. That world was far from the boring confines of Cesar Chavez High School and the dreary *barrio*. And that world did not include Ernesto. She had to be dreaming of gigs in Vegas.

Orlando sang two songs after Naomi's number. And the band played a few instrumentals. Then the show was over.

Ernesto walked to the Volvo in the darkness to wait for Naomi. Suddenly she emerged into the light. She wore the blue pullover and jeans she had on before the show She carried a dark green garbage bag. Ernesto didn't know what was in it.

She seemed about to say something. But then Felix and Linda Martinez came over to hug their daughter. "You were so beautiful, baby!" her father exclaimed. "And you sang like an angel."

"I could hardly believe it was you," her mother told her. "I've always known you were beautiful and you could sing good, but tonight!"

"I was proud of you, Sis," Zack said.

"Thanks," Naomi said to her parents and brother.

Then she turned and looked at Ernesto. He thought, "Was she wondering why he too wasn't saying something complimentary about her performance?" She looked almost angry. Ernesto was more scared than ever. Was she already a diva, enraged that her boyfriend was not lavishing praise on her as her parents and brother were? Maybe she was thinking of a way to tell Ernesto something important. The minute classes ended for the year, she was joining the Oscar Perez band. He wouldn't be seeing too much of her until September when their senior year started. Maybe, Ernesto thought, he was too lame for Naomi now.

The Martinez family walked off, and Naomi turned to Ernesto. "Where are we parked?" she almost barked.

"Over there," Ernesto said, pointing to the Volvo. Ernesto felt like a Volvo at the moment—boring, unexciting, ugly. He walked toward the car. Naomi marched beside him, carrying her garbage bag. When Ernesto opened the passenger side of the car, she got in, tossing the bag onto the back seat. She leaned back and closed her eyes as Ernesto started the car.

"I could puke," Naomi declared.

"What?" Ernesto gasped.

"Let's go somewhere and have some coffee," Naomi commanded.

Ernesto didn't know what to say except, "Okay, sure." Then he asked, "What's in the bag?"

"My stupid, idiotic dress," Naomi answered. "I felt like a freak. It was too tight. I could hardly breathe. Oh man! Nobody's ever gonna talk me into anything like that again. I thought I'd burst out of the stupid front part of that dress. One of the drummers in the band made some gross remark about it. Orlando threatened to kill him! What a night!"

"You . . . uh . . . looked beautiful," Ernesto commented.

"I did not!" Naomi almost screamed at Ernesto. "I looked like I'd been poured into that dress! Ernie, don't make ridiculous, inane comments about it."

"But you sang nice," Ernesto offered, struggling with this totally surprising turn of events.

"I did my best for my brothers' sake," Naomi asserted. "I didn't want to embarrass them. But nobody cared what I sounded like. They just wanted to see a girl in a tight dress, waltzing around the stage. Don't you get it, Ernie? It's not about singing anymore. It's about the girl looking hot. That's why that famous girl singer—if you can call her a singer— that's why she performs from a stripper pole. Never in a million years is anybody ever going to talk me into doing some-thing so stupid again!"

Ernesto was overjoyed, but he didn't want to show his feelings. He didn't want to admit how terrified he was that he was of losing Naomi to the world of showbiz. He didn't want to confess how insecure he felt.

They pulled into a coffee shop and ordered two mochas. They split a huge brownie.

"So what did Orlando and Manny think?" Ernesto asked. He had heard her brothers urging her to join them in the band, at least for the summer.

"You mean after Orlando tried to strangle the drummer for his comments about me?" Naomi snapped. She growled better than Brutus on his worst day.

"Well . . ." Ernesto said, sipping his mocha and nibbling on his half of the brownie.

"It's just totally not my thing, Ernie," Naomi swore. "I'm glad my brothers are en-joying their music. Orlando has a beautiful voice, and I love to hear him sing. Dad does too. And Manny is getting better on the guitar all the time. I think they've found their niche. But, Ernie, I'm not a good singer. I'm okay, but I'm not like my brothers. They're really into music. The only way I fit into that scene is with too much makeup and a really tight dress. I hate that. It makes me feel like a trained seal or something. Like everybody is thinking, 'She can't sing, but oh baby!'"

"Well . . . ," Ernesto said. He wasn't doing well on feedback for the moment.

"One of the guys in the band told me I should wear shorts for the next performance," Naomi snorted.

"What did Orlando say about that?" Ernesto asked.

"Luckily he didn't hear it. He was too busy trying to kill the drummer," Naomi responded.

"Okay," Ernesto thought. "Maybe she might be done talking about her performance."

"So," he said out loud to Naomi, changing the subject, "what about Zack? Did your father and Zack get everything squared away."

Naomi seemed content to talk about something else. "Yeah," she answered. "We had a big family discussion. Mom, as usual, said nothing. Orlando did most of the talking. I did my share too. Zack made his case for wanting to be Daddy's clone. The talk was kinda poignant, really. I think Dad was kinda touched. Here's this big, good-looking eighteen-year-old guy, and his father is his hero! Dad said he'd get Zack into the apprentice program. He'd start out working with guys like Dad's friend Eppy. Then Zack could work his way up. Zack looked so happy. They bought his hard hat already. You can't even get on the construction site without a hard hat. So Zack's got it. He kept trying it on, smiling."

"Wow, that's something," Ernesto said.

"Yeah, Monday morning they'll both climb in the pickup, and they'll go off together. It's actually kinda cute," Naomi remarked.

"I'm glad for Zack," Ernesto commented. "He was so miserable in college. Nobody should have to do something they hate."

"Yeah," Naomi agreed. "I remember you encouraging Abel to follow his dream. You gave him the courage to admit he wanted to be a chef. Now he's so happy working on that. That's the only way anybody has a shot at being happy. Not somebody else's dream for you, but your own dream."

"You figure out what your dream is yet, Naomi?" Ernesto asked.

"Oh, I'm kicking some ideas around," she answered. "I'm pretty good in math and science. Ms. Osborne, my math teacher, she's giving me an A. And Mr. Cabral, he talked to me and said I could maybe be an engineer. I was kinda excited about that."

"Maybe you'll be an engineer designing big projects. Then your dad and Zack'll be working on them," Ernesto suggested. "Wouldn't that be cool?"

"That'd be funny," Naomi chuckled. "But who knows? Engineering seems so cold. I don't think I'd enjoy it. There has to be something else for me, something that really excites me." She finished her mocha and her half of the brownie. "I know one thing. No more slinky dresses and singing. That is totally for the birds."

Ernesto smiled. He couldn't have hoped for a better outcome.

As they walked to the Volvo, Naomi remarked, "You didn't really say much about how I did at Hortencia's, Ernie. Just for the fun of it, what did you *really* think?"

"Uh, you were, you know . . . good," Ernesto replied.

"Come on, Ernie," she demanded. "We're too close for you to fake it. You had the weirdest look on your face when I showed up with my stupid dress in the garbage bag. What were you really thinking when you saw me up there on stage? You can tell me. Be honest. I can take it."

"I wanted to puke," Ernesto responded, ineptly.

"What?" Naomi gasped.

"Yeah," he nodded. "Not because you weren't good, babe. You were all that, and you have a slammin' voice. I thought your performance was great. In fact, I thought you were so good that I was terrified. I thought you'd want a big career. Maybe you wouldn't want to hang around with me anymore."

Ernesto fiddled with the keys to the Volvo. "I coulda puked because I was so scared. I looked at that gorgeous girl on the stage. Then I looked around at all those dudes whistling and stamping their feet. I thought, 'How is dull old Ernie Sandoval gonna compete with *that*?'"

"Oh baby," Naomi responded. "Let me tell you something. Nothing in the world could take me away from Ernie Sandoval. You're more exciting to me than that whole roomful of people."

She stood on tiptoe and kissed Ernesto for good measure.

CHAPTER SIX

Ernesto went to bed happy that night. He went into a very sound sleep, maybe the soundest sleep in a week. No pressing problems weighed on his mind. All was peaceful at the Martinez household. Naomi loved him. Nothing could be better. Ernesto had been chosen senior class president. He was excited thinking about all he planned to do in his senior year.

Then, in the middle of the night, Ernesto heard his mother yelling. Maria Sandoval was not the sort of a woman who yelled for no good reason, especially not at two in the morning.

"Honestly," Mom yelled, "guys are so impatient! I mean, when they are ready to do something, they want to do it right away! Ernie was the same way! Katalina and Juanita were right on time. They arrived at a decent hour! It looks like Alfredo is going to be the same way as Ernie!"

Ernesto sat up in bed. He leaped out of bed, threw his robe on, and raced to his parents' room. Mom's bag was already packed. She had packed it a week ago. Dad was out in the garage starting the car.

"Mom," Ernesto gasped, "is it time?"

Mom was still in bed. She winced and managed a smile. "Two weeks early, but on his time schedule, yeah."

"Should I come with you guys?" Ernesto offered. He remembered when Juanita came, six years ago. He was ten years old. The neighbor lady came over to stay with Ernesto and Katalina. Ernesto recalled being excited then.

"No, no, Ernie," Mom directed. "Your job and *Abuela*'s is to stay with the girls. You tell them where we are when they get up." Ernesto nodded yes.

His Dad came back to their room. Ernesto picked up his mother's bag and took it out to the garage.

Luis Sandoval was fully dressed. He wore jeans and a windbreaker. He gently helped Mom get up from the bed and change into street clothes. They walked carefully to the car. Dad put Mom in the passenger side, carefully buckling her in. Then he ran around to the driver's side.

Ernesto leaned in the window and gave his mother a kiss. The last thing she said was, "I'll call you guys when Alfredo comes. Or your father will call. Depends . . . "

Ernesto stood in the driveway of the house on Wren Street and watched his parents' car disappear into the night. Ernesto turned to see *Abuela* standing in the doorway.

"They're off," she declared.

"Yeah, the baby wasn't due for a while yet," Ernesto said.

"You can't time them like eggs," *Abuela* said. "They come when they come."

Ernesto and his grandmother sat in the kitchen for a while. *Abuela* made coffee for herself. Ernesto poured a large glass of milk.

"When I had my oldest, Magda, they kept us in the hospital for ten days," *Abuela* recalled. "They kept women too long. It's better now. The mother and baby come home quickly. Right away almost, if there are no complications."

Ernesto focused on the word—"complications." He didn't like it. Mom was radiantly healthy. In all her prenatal visits, her doctor was delighted with her progress. The baby was developing perfectly. There was no reason to expect complications. Yet Ernesto was nervous. He was glad Mr. Martinez had given him the new cell phone with his regular number. Mom or Dad could get him wherever he was.

"Ernie," *Abuela* remarked, "you mustn't stay up all night. You must get your rest. Why don't you try to get some sleep? I'll wake you up if I hear anything. Sometimes, you know, a mother can be in the hospital for hours. Your mother waited for over three hours before you decided to enter the world."

"No, it's okay," Ernesto responded. "I couldn't sleep if I tried." He paused and then said, *"Three hours?* Really?" Ernesto hoped Mom wouldn't have to wait so long for Alfredo.

"Just a couple of hours with Katalina," *Abuela* added, as if reading Ernesto's mind. "And Juanita was almost born in the car."

"Oh yeah, I remember Mom telling us that," Ernesto recollected. He gulped his milk. Now he was hoping Alfredo wouldn't be born in the car.

As they sat at the kitchen table, *Abuela* filled the time telling stories from the past. They were stories about when she was a child or when Dad was growing up. She was trying to keep Ernesto listening to her so that he wouldn't worry.

At 4 o'clock the phone rang. Ernesto jumped up and grabbed it so fast he almost fell over his own feet.

"Alfredo came," Dad announced.

"Is Mom okay?" Ernesto almost shouted into the phone.

"She's fine. Alfredo is screaming his head off," Dad reported. He sounded happy.

Ernesto talked to his mother for a few minutes. Then he rushed into his sisters' room to give them the news.

"Alfredo was just born," Ernesto cried, grabbing both girls in a hug. "Our little brother is here, and Mom is doing great!"

"Where?" Juanita screamed. "Where is he?"

"He's in the hospital with Mom and Dad," *Abuela* explained.

"As soon as the hospital has visiting hours," Ernesto promised, "we'll all drive down to see Mom. All four of us will go see Mom and baby Alfredo. Then she'll be home with the baby in no time."

About midmorning on Sunday, Ernesto, *Abuela*, and the girls piled into the Volvo. Off they went to visit Mom and Alfredo.

When Ernesto, *Abuela*, and his sisters came into Mom's room, Mom was sitting up in bed. Ernesto thought she never looked so beautiful. Ernesto and his sisters kissed their mother.

"The nurse is bringing Alfredo in a few minutes," Mom told them. "I called Mom and Dad. They're on their way down here. Me and Alfredo should be going home tomorrow."

In a few minutes, the nurse came with the baby. Katalina and Juanita gazed on him in wonder. They'd never seen a new baby in their family before.

"He's so little," Juanita remarked.

"And reddish," Katalina noted.

"Look," Ernesto said, "he's got lots of hair already, like me."

"He's beautiful, isn't he?" Dad asked, coming around the corner. He sat on the bed and snuggled with Mom. "Good job, babe," he whispered.

The little house on Wren Street wasn't big enough for a nursery. The Sandovals had partitioned off a corner of their bedroom for the baby's crib. They wanted the baby close to them during the early months.

Mom and the baby came home on the next day, Monday. Maria's parents arrived at the Sandoval house in the late afternoon. Mr. and Mrs. Sandoval bustled them right off to the crib in their bedroom. *Abuela* Eva rushed into the room.

"Ohhh!" Eva Vasquez cooed. "Such a lovely baby! It's a shame he doesn't have a nursery room of his own. It seems so cramped in here."

"It's perfect, Mama," Ernesto's mother assured her. "It's cozy. We want to be close to our baby. We don't want him off in another room when he's so small."

Alfredo Vasquez, Maria Sandoval's father, had remained standing in the doorway of the room. Now he entered slowly.

Abuelo Alfredo usually had very little to say. He wasn't openly emotional as a rule. He let his wife do the talking—and she did. They'd been that way during their entire marriage. When his only child, Maria, had her first son, they named the boy Ernesto. Alfredo had never complained about that. But deep in his heart, he thought how nice it would have been if his daughter's son was named for him. Then Katalina and Juanita were born. It didn't seem like Alfredo's daughter would ever have another son. But then Maria Sandoval was expecting her second son. And she promised her father he would be named Alfredo, for him.

Now *Abuelo* Alfredo made his way into the room and peered into the crib with damp eyes. "What a handsome little boy," he commented. "Look at those bright eyes. And nice hair already. I'm sure it's only my imagination. But Eva, don't you think he looks a bit like me around the eyes?"

Eva Vasquez was about to say that he was being ridiculous. Such a tiny baby never looked like anyone yet. But she paused and looked at her husband. Then, in a rare moment of grace, she agreed. "Yes Al, I *do* see a resemblance."

The next Saturday, Ernesto, Paul Morales, and Abel went shopping at the supermarket again for the Lopez family. They were on SNAP and doing better. But they still needed a little extra help. They bought some of the items that were not necessities but that were still important, especially for the little girls. They picked up cookies, nutrition bars, chocolate pudding in little cups, and TV dinners. The dinners would be easy for Mr. Lopez to just pop in the oven for himself, the children, and Beatrice. Mrs. Lopez was not eating much anyway. The chemo and radiation treatments were making Mrs. Lopez very sick. And they weren't helping her much that anyone could see.

The boys pulled up to the Lopez house in Ernesto's Volvo. Naomi's Chevy classic was already there. Another car they didn't recognize was parked in the driveway.

When the boys went in, they saw a middle-aged woman sitting by Beatrice Lopez's bed. Mrs. Lopez had been given a hospital bed. Now she could sit up and lie down just by pushing a button.

Mr. Lopez and Cruz helped unload the groceries. Mr. Lopez thanked them profusely, as usual. Naomi was there. She had just brought some ice cream bars for the girls and put them into the freezer.

"I will be returning to work next week," Mr. Lopez told the boys. "That will bring in money."

Cruz told them he was doing well at his classes at the community college. He was really enjoying the work. "I think I'm gonna make it," Cruz declared. "I'm gonna get the hang of this electrical stuff and make some money."

"That's great, man," Paul told him. "You're on your way. I bet that means a lot to your mom."

"Yeah," Cruz nodded. "I've given her a lot of grief, dude." He shook his head.

Naomi joined the boys and explained in a soft voice, "The lady sitting by Mrs. Lopez is Petra Saldono. She's going

119

to come every day now. She's from . . . hospice."

Naomi swallowed hard. "She's going to make sure Mrs. Lopez is comfortable and she'll put on the pain patches. It's going to be . . . much easier." Naomi swallowed hard again.

"Yeah," Paul said. His voice was thick and unnatural. He walked over and said hello to Mrs. Lopez. She gave him her hand, and he squeezed it gently. She knew how much this young man loved her son. That meant a lot to her.

In a little while, everyone left the Lopez house. Paul Morales walked with Ernesto and Abel to the Volvo. Naomi trailed them to the door. They gathered in the darkened front yard.

"I'm glad you guys brought something," Naomi told the boys. "The girls liked the ice cream bars."

Paul Morales didn't say anything. He climbed into the Volvo with a very sad look on his face. Paul cared a lot for Cruz and his family. Things were looking up now for Cruz and his father, and that was good. Yet a darkness enveloped Paul. Ernesto understood, but neither he nor Abel knew what to say.

They pulled up to Paul's apartment on Cardinal Street. Usually when they dropped Paul off, he hurried to his apartment. Then the car sped off. This time, when they parked, Ernesto and Abel got out. Both boys put their arms around Paul Morales. They hugged him as they would a badly upset child. Paul Morales never had a family of his own, except for his brother David. He had been in a series of foster homes growing up. So when he bonded with Cruz and his family, the bond was deep. They meant more to him than they would have meant to somebody with a good, strong family of his own.

Paul walked toward his apartment.

"He was crying man," Abel gasped. "Paul was crying."

"Yeah," Ernesto acknowledged.

"I guess it was seeing the hospice nurse," Abel commented. "I mean, it's good that she's there for them, but . . . "

"Yeah," Ernesto said. "They usually come at the end."

Ernesto felt bad for Paul Morales. He felt bad for the Lopez family. He felt bad for all the people who suffered in the world. And the awareness of all that suffering engulfed him now in a terrible, almost suffocating way. There was no way to make all that pain go away. But there was a way to ease it in a small way, and they had done that.

At school on Monday, Ernesto noticed Mira Nuñez walking to class alone. She was usually with her boyfriend, Clay Aguirre. Mira did not look happy.

Naomi was with Ernesto, and she noticed Mira's gloomy expression too. "What happened there?" she wondered. "Mira looks like something's really wrong." When Mira got close enough, Naomi called out, "Hi Mira. Everything okay? You look sorta sad."

Mira turned. "Oh, I'm okay I guess," she said halfheartedly. Then she went on. "There's a new junior guy in our class. He's a transfer student from another school. Maybe you've seen him. His name is Kenny Trujillo."

"Yeah, I've seen him. He's in my science class," Naomi said. "He's a pretty nice guy. He jokes around a lot."

"Well," Mira continued, "after class the other day, he gave me a compliment. Clay got mad. All Kenny said was that I really looked good in my jeans. Clay expected me to act all insulted and put the guy in his place and stuff. But Kenny didn't mean anything. Now Clay's all bent out of shape. He won't even talk to me. He's saying I was flirting with Kenny, but I wasn't. I don't even know the guy. I mean, it's no big deal—except to Clay."

Ernesto felt like telling Mira to dump Clay Aguirre for good because there was nothing but trouble ahead. But Ernesto knew that would just hurt Mira's feelings. And she was obviously hurting anyway.

123

"Mom says guys are so hard to under-stand," Mira remarked. "I mean, Mom had this new boyfriend for about four months. They were really close. Mom was starting to think maybe this was *the guy*. Now all of a sudden he isn't answering her phone calls. He's just gone silent on her."

Mira frowned and continued. "Mom said she musta done something to upset him. But she doesn't know what. That's how it is with me and Clay. One little thing just sets him off. Half the time I hardly know what it is."

Naomi had told Ernesto once how Mira's father had left Mira and her mother. All of a sudden, he wasn't happy in the mar-riage anymore. Both Mira and her mother were devastated. They hadn't see the father's departure coming. Naomi thought that his leaving had shaken Mira's faith in the whole idea of love and relationships. That's why she took so much abuse from Clay. She was always on edge about maybe losing him. Her Dad had disappeared so fast and so suddenly. If she wasn't careful, she thought she could lose Clay too. And she cared for him.

"I'm gonna see Clay at lunch," Mira said, brightening. "I made some nice sandwiches for us, the kind he likes. He loves this special salami with the dark mustard, and that's what I made. I even used that rye bread he's so crazy about. I made two sandwiches, one for him and one for me. But he can have both if he's hungry. I think maybe that'll smooth things over." Mira smiled hopefully and walked on.

"Well," Naomi commented to Ernesto, "they say the way to a man's heart is through his stomach. Maybe it'll work. I know my dad is much nicer when Mom makes something he likes, like *carne asada*. When she puts out some veggie dish, he gets kinda grumpy."

"Poor Mira," Ernesto remarked. "She deserves better than that jerk Clay. If I were her, I'd hit him in the head with those sandwiches."

Naomi giggled. "Oh Ernie!"

Then she turned serious. "You know, since she lost the election for senior class president to you Mira told me Clay Aguirre hasn't been as nice to her. He kinda blames her for losing the election. He said she made a dumb speech at the assembly that day. He told her she turned everybody off. But the truth is, you made such a fantastic speech that you won everybody's hearts. Nobody else had a chance, babe."

At lunchtime, Clay Aguirre and Mira Nuñez usually ate together at a spot opposite the science building. Some benches were there. If you arrived early, you could find good shade under the overhanging eucalyptus trees. With warmer weather coming and bright sunlight, shade was a real plus on the Cesar Chavez High School campus.

Ernesto was on his way to meet his friends for lunch. Then he noticed Mira hurrying by with her large brown lunch bag. It looked as though it was filled with those special salami sandwiches.

"Hi Clay," Mira sang out in her sweetest voice. "I made your favorite sandwiches today. I got that salami you like at the deli, and the dark mustard. I found just the right rye bread. It's all in here, babe." She waved her lunch bag toward him.

"Keep your stupid sandwich!" Clay snarled. "How do ya think you made me feel? You flirt with some new jerk you don't even know in front of all my friends. And they know you're my girlfriend? You and that jackass Trujillo were carrying on like idiots. Everybody was laughing at me. Haven't you got any self-respect?"

"Clay, I . . . I wasn't flirting," Mira stammered.

Ernesto thought he was going to be sick just hearing the girl's whiny, abject voice. He wanted to grab Mira by her shoulders and shout at her. "Girl, lose the creep! You deserve better!"

Mira hurried away from Clay, tears streaking down her face. Naomi spotted her and called out, "Hey Mira, come on eat

127

with us." Mira saw Naomi, Carmen, and a couple of other girls. "We're heading for lunch right now. Carmen brought nice blueberry muffins to share. Come on!"

Clay Aguirre glared at Mira and Naomi. He expected Mira to stand there pleading with him a bit longer. Maybe he expected her to degrade herself. If she did, maybe he might have relented and eaten that sandwich. But she gave up too easy. So he walked away.

Mira looked after Clay sadly, still clutching the brown bag. She had looked at about half a dozen salamis in the deli. Finally, she'd found the exact kind he liked. She searched and searched for the odd-shaped bottle of dark mustard that he preferred. She checked out ten loaves of bread, looking for his chewy rye. She lovingly made the sandwiches. She was certain they would end the deep freeze that Clay had her in.

CHAPTER SEVEN

Naomi and Mira walked to the grassy spot where the other three girls waited.

"I got blueberry muffins for everybody," Carmen announced. "They're delicious. They're supposed to be good for you too. Glad you could join us, Mira."

The other girls, Tessie Zamora and Yvette Ozono, greeted Mira too. They all noticed how downcast she was. They asked her why she was so down.

"Me and Clay aren't getting along too good," Mira confessed. She sadly unwrapped one of the salami sandwiches she had hoped to be eating with Clay. "I'm always sorta walking on eggshells with him. It can be going real good. Then some stupid little thing happens to set him off. That new guy, Kenny Trujillo, said I looked good in my jeans. I laughed, and Clay just freaked."

"Kenny's a riot," Tessie remarked. "He's in my English class. He makes everybody laugh. He's a funny guy."

"He seems nice," Mira replied. "I know he didn't mean anything talking about my jeans. But Clay expected me to act real insulted and take his head off."

There was a moment of awkward silence. Then Naomi spoke up. "You guys all know I was with Clay for a long time. We had some really good times. I thought I was in love with him. I mean, Clay can be so charming and nice. But it got to the point that I had to think about everything I said or did. I had to kinda weigh how he would look at whatever I did. That got really old."

"Yeah," Mira said. "That's how it is with me and Clay. I can't say just what I'm thinking because he might take it the wrong way."

Carmen chimed in. "You know my boyfriend, Paul Morales, he's kind of a bad boy. He's going to the community college, and my dad doesn't like him much."

Tessie giggled. "He hangs out with homies. He's got a rattlesnake tattooed on his hand. Oooooo!"

"Yeah," Carmen said. "Paul's had a rough childhood and stuff, but I don't care what I say to him. You guys all know I talk too much. I can say anything to Paul, and he just laughs. I go on and on, and Paul sorta grimaces. Then asks me if I don't ever take a breath. I punch him in the shoulder and just keep on talking. I'm never scared that he's gonna be mad or anything. I couldn't stand to be with a guy who's real touchy like that."

"I know where Mira's coming from," Naomi added. "I put up with Clay for a long time. I just couldn't break with him 'cause I cared too much for him. I look back on it now, and I think I must have been crazy. But at the time it made sense. You guys all know why I finally cut him loose. I've told you Carmen, Yvette, Tessie, but I didn't tell you, Mira." Naomi turned her gaze toward Mira. "Did Clay ever say anything to about why we broke up?"

"Clay told me you guys were sort of fighting. He accidentally elbowed you in the face or something," Mira replied.

"No," Naomi asserted. "Clay punched me in the face. We were with a bunch of people. I complimented Ernie about how good he was looking since he was lifting weights. I hardly knew Ernie then. He'd just come down from LA. Anyway, Clay went nuts. Before the night was over, he punched me in the face. Boy, that was a wake-up call for me. I finally had to face the truth that me and Clay were over."

"I don't have a boyfriend now," Tessie interjected. "But I wouldn't want to be with anybody who wasn't nice. I'd rather be alone any day than have some mean dude in my life."

All this time, Yvette Ozono had been very quiet. Now she looked very sad and she finally spoke. "I hung out for a long time with a gangbanger named Coyote. He was horrible to me, but I thought I didn't deserve any better. Then I found a nice guy, Tommy Alvarado, but Coyote killed him. I about died. I wanted to be in the casket with Tommy. I didn't want to wake up in the morning. Then Ernie and his father helped me to come back to school and to be happy again. Now I got a nice boyfriend, Phil Serra. I'm telling you, Mira, having a mean boyfriend just ruins your whole life. It makes everything dark and scary."

"Yvette is right," Naomi confirmed. "Everybody has a right to be treated decently. Ernie is the sweetest guy. When I'm with him, there's no fear. That's how it ought to be."

Mira looked forlorn. "I'd hate for me and Clay to break up," she sighed. "I wish that Kenny Trujillo had just left me alone. Then everything woulda been okay."

The other girls looked at one another, shaking their heads.

The girls finished their lunches. They got up and brushed the grass clippings off their jeans. Carmen's phone rang. "Yeah, Paul," she said. Immediately a stricken look came to Carmen's face.

"What's the matter, Carmen?" Naomi asked. "What's wrong?"

"They took Mrs. Lopez to the hospital," Carmen reported. "Paul said Mr. Lopez's mother came down from San Fernando to be with the girls. Mrs. Lopez is really bad. She's like in a coma."

After school, Carmen rode with Paul Morales down to the hospital. Paul wanted to be with his friend, Cruz, to support him. Ernesto Sandoval drove Naomi down too. When they got there, they spotted Abel Ruiz's car and Beto Ortiz's green van.

Ernesto and Naomi came into Mrs. Lopez's room. Padre Benito had finished anointing her. Paul and Carmen stood near the woman's bed. Cruz, Beto, and Abel were nearby also. Andrea and Sarah Lopez were down in the cafeteria with their grandmother. Mr. Lopez sat in the chair at his wife's bedside, his face ashen.

Ernesto looked at the woman lying in the bed. She had never been a large woman. But now she was almost shrunken to the size of a child. Her eyes were closed, and she was breathing unevenly. She had no tubes connected to her, as they had been before. She had been given morphine for the pain. Her hands were clasped over her chest. Rosary beads were entwined in her fingers.

Ernesto's gaze met Paul's. They shared a heartbroken look. They both felt the sadness. But there was nothing to say. Cruz walked over and knelt at his father's chair. He grasped his father's hands. The grandmother came into the room with the two daughters. They weren't crying, but they looked grief stricken. Both of the girls, first Andrea and then Sarah, leaned over their mother's bed. Each whispered, "I love you, Mama."

The grandmother told them, "She heard you. Even though she seems not to hear, she heard you. The nurse said the hearing is the last to go."

Miguel Lopez kissed his wife. He told her in Spanish how much he loved her. He took her hands in his and clung to them. He lifted them to his lips and kissed them, again and again.

Before long, Luis and Maria Sandoval arrived. They came with Emilio Ibarra and his wife, Conchita. Felix Martinez and Linda came with their son, Zack. Felix Martinez and Emilio Ibarra had been enemies when Ibarra defeated Martinez's cousin for city council. Now the men shook hands and stood somberly together in the room.

Beatrice Lopez died at four thirty in the afternoon. She just quietly stopped breathing. The room filled with sobs from everyone.

Long into the night, people filled the Lopezes' small apartment. Maria Sandoval and Abel Ruiz cooked for the family and the others. Paul and Beto sat with Cruz and talked. It was almost midnight before most of the friends and neighbors went home. Then Mr. Lopez was alone with his son and two daughters. Paul Morales and Beto Ortiz spent the night with them. They lay on the floor in sleeping bags.

Paul had to be with Cruz to comfort him after the loss of his mother. Paul had lost his mother too. That had been many years ago, when he was a small boy. But Paul never really knew the drug-addicted woman who was his mother. Beatrice Lopez had been a warm and loving mother. She had always done her best for her husband and children. It was harder for Cruz to lose her than it had been for Paul.

At school the following day, Naomi hurried to talk to Ernesto. She had something important to say.

"I'm going to apply for advanced placement biology in my senior year," Naomi told him.

"That's great, Naomi," Ernesto said. "That'll be a hard class."

"I've done really well in science this year," Naomi explained. "And I've made

137

up my mind what I'm going to do." Naomi's face showed a determination that Ernesto had not seen before. Whenever Ernesto had asked Naomi about her dreams for the future, she had always seemed uncertain. She had been unfocused. "You know why, Ernie?" Naomi asked. Her beautiful violet eyes shone with fervor. "Beatrice Lopez gave me a gift last night."

Ernesto didn't know what to say. All the while he and Naomi had been in the hospital room, Mrs. Lopez had not been responsive. Ernesto hadn't seen the woman speak a word to Naomi or to anybody else. How could she have given Naomi a gift?

"Ernie," Naomi continued, her voice trembling a little. "That beautiful woman . . . she wasn't even forty. I looked at her, and I looked at her children. I thought it wasn't right that she died."

At first, Ernesto didn't get what Naomi meant. Mr. Lopez had worked for a construction company. The boss had discouraged Mrs. Lopez from getting medical treatment. The treatments caused the company's insurance premiums to go up. So Mrs. Lopez didn't go to the doctors when they might have saved her life. Paul Morales had been very angry about that. Ernesto thought Naomi was angry about that too.

Then Naomi continued speaking. "When I was a little girl, I read a book about Marie Curie. She won Nobel Prizes for physics and chemistry. I remember thinking how that woman made such a difference. But I didn't think much about it after that. Last night, when I was with Beatrice Lopez, I thought about Marie Curie. I wondered, 'What if I went into medical research? I could dedicate my work to her. Maybe I could discover something so that another person wouldn't have to die like that.' That's what I'm going to do, Ernie. There's so much incredible medical research going on right now. I want to be a part of that when I graduate from college. I want to do research in a laboratory.

Maybe someday another young woman like Beatrice Lopez can be cured and live a normal lifetime."

Ernesto took Naomi in his arms and hugged her. "Babe, that's beautiful," he responded. "It's exciting and wonderful. I know you'll make a big difference someday."

"Until now, whenever I thought of another career," Naomi told him, "I thought, 'Well, maybe.' But now I'm sure about this."

"Well, I guess we both got dreams to chase now, Naomi," Ernesto declared. "We can chase them together."

The funeral for Beatrice Lopez was held four days later at Our Lady of Guadalupe Church. Padre Benito presided at her funeral. As a young priest, he had married Miguel and Beatrice Lopez. And he had christened all their children.

Nobody expected many people to come to the funeral. The Lopez family had always lived in small apartments in the *barrio*. But they had few close friends.

They were always a little poorer than their neighbors. Beatrice Lopez was embarrassed to have visitors. So they stayed pretty much to themselves.

But the little church was overflowing with people. Many beautiful bouquets of flowers adorned the altar. In the first pew were Mr. Lopez, Cruz, his grandmother, and the girls. Paul Morales sat beside Cruz. Councilman Emilio Ibarra, his wife Conchita, and their children sat with them. In the second pew sat the rest of the Sandoval family with the Martinez family. The Ruiz family came along with the Ortiz family.

Cruz looked as though his world had crashed. He seemed to be taking the loss of his mother worse than even his father was. Ernesto knew that Miguel Lopez felt as though he'd let his wife down. He could have taken his wife for treatment earlier. But he had not stuck up for his rights with his employer. He had been tricked into thinking he had no coverage. Cruz, though, was feeling even worse than his father.

Over the past several years, he had made his mother worry so much about him.

Later, Ernesto learned that Councilman Ibarra was paying for most of the funeral. The rest was covered by contributions from several other families, including the Sandovals and the Martinezes.

Beatrice Lopez was laid to rest at Holy Cross Cemetery. Afterward, the Sandovals, Ibarras, and Martinezes went home with Mr. Lopez and his family. They went in and helped Miguel Lopez's mom make dinner. Paul and Beto took a drive with Cruz. Carmen did the driving at the wheel of her car. What Cruz needed more than anything was the support of his best friend. Ernesto could tell that Carmen Ibarra was out of her element. She had lived a much better life than the three boys in her car. But she was wanted to help Paul.

CHAPTER EIGHT

The next time Naomi and Ernesto saw Mira Nuñez at school, she still seemed to be having trouble with Clay Aguirre.

"I guess the jerk is still holding it against Mira," Ernesto remarked. "And all she did was get a compliment from that dude Trujillo."

Naomi shook her head. "Look at her moping around like a little puppy. She's heading for the vending machine. Uh-oh, here comes Clay. He's going there too. Maybe this is the big moment when they get back together."

"I almost hope not," Ernesto said. "It would be so good for Mira if Clay just vanished from her life. Right now it would hurt. But she'd be much better off in the long run."

"Ernie!" Naomi gasped. "There's Kenny Trujillo! He's spotted Mira. He's going over to the vending machine too. The poor guy! He's walking into a buzz saw, and he doesn't even know it. You think we should warn him?"

"Trujillo's gonna get there before Clay, Naomi," Ernesto replied. "It's too late. The poor dude has his eye on Mira. She's a cute chick, and he's got ideas!"

Ernesto and Naomi couldn't take their eyes off the scene. Mira stood before the vending machine, trying to decide what she wanted. She had no idea of what was about to go down. She was just looking at those luscious-looking pears that had just arrived. Or should she pick one of the bright red apples that she liked so well?

"The pears are awesome," Kenny Trujillo commented, reaching Mira's side. "Get a pear, girl. You won't be sorry. I got one of those yesterday, and it was incredible."

Clay Aguirre stopped cold in his tracks. He stared at them at the vending machine. Had Clay been heading toward Mira to finally make up with her? Or had he planned to just walk past her again, continuing to torment her with the silent treatment. Naomi knew his routine all too well. Clay could keep the silent treatment going for days or, when he was really mad, even for weeks. Naomi remembered when Clay would give her the cold shoulder. When they finally made up, she thought she was in heaven. That was how Clay kept his girlfriend in line.

"Oh," Mira responded, "those pears *do* look good."

Clay was standing about twenty feet away. His face was filled with rage.

"The pears are sweet and delectable," Kenny flirted. "Like you."

Clay reached the vending machine in a few long strides. "Hey Trujillo," he snarled. "What's your problem?"

"Problem?" Kenny asked, startled. "I got no problem, dude. I was just recommending the pears. Who're you anyway?"

"This is my girlfriend, pig face," Clay growled. Kenny Trujillo didn't look at all like a pig. But it was the first insult Clay could think of. Kenny was not handsome, but he was nice looking. He had friendly brown eyes and a ready smile. "What's with you, man, harassing my girlfriend?"

"Harassing?" Kenny repeated. He seemed annoyed but not angered. He was a laid-back guy. Clay Aguirre was agitated. His eyes narrowed, and his skin grew red. "Look dude, I don't know what's with you. I wasn't harassing anybody. The mental health clinic is just down the street, though. It might do you some good."

Clay reached for Mira's hand and jerked her away from the vending machine. "Come on, babe, you don't have to be harassed by some jerk," Clay sneered. Clay reacted as if the silent treatment of the past week had never happened. The two seemed as close as ever. "This monkey won't be bothering you again. Unless he wants to deal with me." Clay looked at Kenny with pure hatred. "Stay away from this chick, man," he threatened, "unless you want a fat lip." Clay practically dragged Mira away.

Kenny Trujillo looked dumbfounded. Naomi and Ernesto walked over to him. "Hi, I'm Ernie. This is Naomi," Ernesto made the introductions. "We're juniors here at Chavez too. You're the new kid on the block. So we need to defend the reputation of our school. We only got a few idiots, and you just met one. You're Kenny Trujillo, right?"

"Hi," Kenny responded. "Yeah, that's me. What's with that guy? Did he just escape from a locked facility?"

Ernesto laughed. "No, he's just real jealous. You know, they say if you can't say something nice about someone, say nothing at all. But in this case, I gotta say something. The guy you just met—Clay Aguirre—is a creep. There's no other way to put it."

"Wow!" Kenny exclaimed. "What's a nice chick like her doing with him?"

"He plays football," Naomi explained. "He really looks good in his football uniform. Mira loves that. She thinks football players are hot. I'm not one to throw stones though. I used to date Clay myself."

"The guy isn't dangerous, is he?" Kenny asked.

"Only to girls," Naomi replied. "I complimented a guy once." She glanced and smiled at Ernesto. "Clay got jealous and punched me in the face."

"*He punched you in the face?*" Kenny gasped.

"Yeah," Naomi said. "That's when I dropped him like a hot rock."

Paul Morales called Ernesto on Friday night. "Hey Ernie," Paul said, "me and Cruz and Abel and Beto are goin' out to the desert tomorrow. We're gonna do a little hikin'. Cruz really needs to get his mind off stuff, you know? Wanna come along? We'll

148

all be goin' in Beto's van. Abel's cooking us up great lunches."

The weekend weather was supposed to be cool but bright and sunny. There had been enough rain for the wildflowers to be blooming in the Anza-Borrego Desert.

Ernesto could think of many things he'd rather be doing on Saturday. Hiking in the Anza-Borrego Desert wasn't one of them, even if the wildflowers had come out. But Paul was struggling to cheer Cruz up. So Ernesto figured it was his duty to help. Cruz had just gotten into technical classes at the community college. If he slipped into a funk over losing his mother, he might just dump school. He had done that before. He might slip into his bad old ways. He used to just hang on the streets with the other gang wannabes.

"Sure Paul, I'll be there," Ernesto agreed. "What should I bring?"

"Just yourself, man," Paul answered. "Everything's covered. Abel did all the food, and we got sodas and stuff. We'll pick you up at your place around ten in the morning. We should be home by dark. Hey, thanks Ernie. Thanks for helpin' out. Cruz's hanging by a thread right now."

"I know," Ernesto said. He felt real sorry for Cruz. Ernesto couldn't even imagine how he'd feel if something happened to either of his parents. Cruz was a tough kid. But losing a parent was an awful thing to deal with.

"You're going hiking in the desert?" Mom asked when Ernesto told her. Her eyebrows shot up.

"Yeah," Ernesto explained, "just at the edge of the Anza-Borrego. We'll park the van, eat, and look at a few wildflowers."

"Can I come too?" Juanita asked. Juanita wasn't exactly jealous of Alfredo, the new baby. But Mom *was* spending an awful lot of time with him. Before Alfredo came home from the hospital, Juanita was the baby of the family. She had always enjoyed that status. "I could come, Ernie. I wouldn't be any trouble."

"Don't be silly," Katalina chimed in scornfully. "A bunch of guys don't want a whiny little girl along."

"I'm *not* a whiny little girl," Juanita snapped.

"Sweetheart," Mom intervened, "Ernie and his friends are going to be doing guy stuff. It wouldn't be any fun for you."

"Yeah, we're gonna be looking for rattlesnakes," Ernesto told the girl. His comment was a misguided effort to discourage Juanita from wanting to come. But the moment he said it, he regretted. Mom's eyebrows went up even higher.

"You are going to be doing *what*?" she cried.

"I was just kidding," Ernesto responded hastily.

"Well, you just be careful," Mom commanded. Alfredo was crying, and Mom went to tend him.

Juanita whined, "He's *always* making a fuss!" She had a dark look on her face.

At ten the next morning, the green van pulled up on Wren Street. Beto was at the wheel. Like Cruz, he too was letting his hair grow in. He wanted to look less like a gangbanger. Paul was beside Beto. Ernesto sat in the back seats with Cruz and Abel.

When they were in the van, Ernesto asked Cruz, "How's it going, man?"

"Grandma's real good with my sisters," Cruz reported. "She's helping a lot. Dad went back to work. So he'll be getting a paycheck now. We can pay the utilities finally." Cruz's voice was upbeat, but his eyes were pools of despair.

Beto remarked, "Cruz's missin' his mom a lot."

Cruz didn't deny it. He slumped in the seat and commented, "The house, it's real strange without her. She, you know, used to be the life of our family. She was always laughin' and huggin' us. Then she got sick. I mean, even then, when she first got sick, she tried to be our mom. She tried, as long as she could. I mean, any fool could see what was comin'."

Cruz dropped his head to his chest. "But I tried to deny it. I tried not to think about it, you know. I thought the medicine would make her better somehow." The others all heard a catch in Cruz's voice. "I see her stuff still layin' all around. Her dresses are in the closet, her shoes . . . "

"You got a girlfriend, Cruz?" Ernesto asked.

"Nah," Cruz replied. "I been out with chicks, but they don't dig me. A chick's scrapin' the bottom of the barrel to wanna hang with me."

"Come on!" Abel exclaimed. "You're not a bad-looking dude. You're just kinda shy, like me. It took me a long time to work up enough courage to get close to Claudia. But now it's great."

"I been talkin' to a girl down in the electrician class at the college," Beto admitted. "I ain't asked her out yet, but maybe soon. You'll find somebody too, Cruz."

"No," Cruz snapped. "I don't want no girlfriend. Chicks just cause more problems. I'd rather be alone. I didn't even wanna come today. I'd rather be someplace by myself."

Paul exchanged a look with Ernesto. The look said, "This guy's in big trouble. He needs help bad."

"I was almost mad at her at the funeral," Cruz confessed. "I looked at her layin' in that casket. She looked so peaceful. I was mad at her for leavin' us. I know that's crazy. She didn't want to leave us." Cruz closed his eyes. He looked terrible. Ernesto hadn't realized the guy was this bad off.

Ernesto wondered whether going out to the desert was such a good idea. What good would staring at wildflowers and sand do the dude? Maybe they should have taken him to a movie with wild special effects. That seemed like it would take his mind off things.

The green van reached the Anza-Borrego Desert. Beto headed for a specific place where he and Paul planned to park. Ernesto figured they had been here many times before. They must have had a favorite spot.

"Look, some people already here," Paul Morales pointed as Beto parked the van. "But they're way over there. They won't bother us. They got a pickup and a little travel trailer looks like."

"You can have a lot of fun in the desert, and it's free," Paul remarked. "Remember, Cruz? This is where we came that day the rattlesnake got me?"

"Yeah," Cruz murmured.

The four boys hiked with Cruz for about an hour. They found some scarlet flowers in the cactus plants. Cruz seemed listless.

Abel was alone with Ernesto for a few minutes. He remarked, "Oh man, I hope this works."

Ernesto looked at Abel, "You hope *what* works?" So far, Ernesto thought, Cruz had been like a zombie.

They returned to the van, and Abel started taking out sandwiches. Ernesto and

Beto and Paul unloaded the ice chest with the sodas. Ernesto glanced over at the travel trailer. A girl in shorts had come out. She seemed to be looking over at the boys. She looked about eighteen or nineteen. She had long, straight hair and large dark eyes. She watched the five boys putting their food out. She wandered over to them. "Hi you guys," she hailed. "Got anything good to eat?"

"Yeah," Abel answered, "I made everything. I'm training to be a chef. Everything I make is good. We got barbecued chicken sandwiches here. And honey ham bagels and roast beef pocket sandwiches. We got hot chicken subs too."

"Whoa!" the girl exclaimed. She glanced at the five boys. "Looks like you got it covered."

Ernesto didn't know what was going on. But he was pretty sure meeting this girl was no accident. When Paul and Beto exchanged a knowing look, Ernesto was even more sure.

"Thanks," Paul responded, introducing the girl to the other four boys. "We're not related, but we're *hermanos* in our hearts."

"I'm Dorotea Alcanar," the girl told them. "Me and my dad're camping here for the weekend." She was pretty. "My friends call me Doro, and my enemies call me Dodo."

A man about fifty, with a silvery, bristly beard, looked out the door of the travel trailer. "Hey boys!" he shouted to them. His daughter was talking to five strange young men who had arrived in a ratty-looking green van. He didn't seem very concerned. Ernesto thought the guy had to be weird.

"You wouldn't want to share some of those sandwiches with us, would you?" Dorotea asked.

"Name your poison," Abel responded.

"Chicken sub for me and roast beef for Pop," Doro ordered. She ran to the travel trailer to deliver her father's sandwich. Then she returned to the boys, who had started eating. She sat down with them as if she'd known them all her life. "Oh," she

157

cried, "this chicken sub is delish. What did you put in it to make it so good—you're Abel, right?"

"Yeah," Abel replied. "I put in yogurt, dill weed, mustard, and alfalfa sprouts. Makes a difference, huh?"

"I bet you got a girlfriend, huh?" Doro asked.

"Yeah," Abel grinned.

Dorotea looked at Ernesto. "You're so cute. You must have a chick."

"Yeah," Ernesto answered. He couldn't figure this girl out. He didn't know exactly what was going on, but it was something strange.

"I'm nineteen," Dorotea announced between bites of chicken sub. "But I don't have a boyfriend yet." Her eyes scanned Paul, Beto, and Cruz. "You all have girlfriends, right?"

"He doesn't," Beto said, pointing to Cruz.

Cruz didn't say anything. He was looking off into the distance. He looked as though he badly wanted to be someplace else. Ernesto thought this was not one of Paul's better ideas. It was not making Cruz feel better. It was only making him feel worse.

Ernesto wished they'd finish eating, pile back into the van, and go home.

Dorotea looked at Cruz. "What did you say your name was?"

"I didn't say," Cruz replied. He didn't look at the girl.

"His name's Cruz Lopez," Beto answered for him. "He just lost his mother, and he's feeling pretty bad."

"Oh, I'm so sorry!" Dorotea cried. "That's gotta be rough."

"It's okay," Cruz snapped, getting up. He stuffed his hands in his pockets and walked a few steps away from the group.

Dorotea got up and followed Cruz. She drew closer to him. She reached out and caressed his cheek with her soft hand. "Poor guy," she sighed.

CHAPTER NINE

Cruz moved away from Dorotea and turned his back to her.

"Let's take a little walk, Cruz," she suggested. "Just you and me. I can show you some amazing flowers."

"Not interested," Cruz snapped.

"I'm lonely too, Cruz," she told him. "It's just me and my pop. We come out to the desert sometimes and that helps. But I'm lonely too. Won't you just take a little walk with me? I'd feel better if you did."

"I don't care," Cruz sighed. "If you want, we can walk. I don't care one way or another."

Ernesto stared at the girl. Her long black silky hair was blowing in the soft desert wind. She reached over and slipped her small hand into Cruz's hand. They began to walk. They found some desert wildflowers. After a few minutes, Cruz asked, "How come it's just you and your father?"

"My parents got divorced a long time ago," Dorotea explained. "Mom raised me. Then she got married again. She's got little kids now with her new husband. My pop, he's just been drifting around like a lost soul. So I thought he needed me. I moved in with him. We have a little apartment, and I got a job. He gets disability from a bad back he got at work. So we make out okay. Sometimes we come out here to camp."

"Don't you miss your mom?" Cruz asked.

"I see her all the time. But she's busy with her new family. She doesn't need me like Pop does. Do you go to school, Cruz?" Dorotea asked.

"Yeah," Cruz replied, "I'm supposed to be learning to be an electrician. I'm at a community college. They got these two-year deals. I don't know if I'll stick it out though. It's hard work. Sometimes I think I'll just drop it and hang out. Maybe I'll take a bus somewhere."

"I bet your mom would want you to stick it out," the girl advised.

Cruz turned sharply and stared at the girl. "You're kinda weird. You don't even know me. You never knew my mom. How do you know what she woulda wanted?" He sounded belligerent.

"I don't know," Dorotea replied, not intimidated. "I think most moms want their kids to get training or some kind of education. Moms want their kids to be able to make their way in the world."

"My mom wanted me to stay in high school, but I wouldn't," Cruz said. "I was a creep."

"No, you're not a creep," Dorotea objected. "I know a creep when I see one. You got a lot of good in you."

"You don't even know me," Cruz snapped. "You don't know all what I done. I dropped high school in the tenth grade. Mom cried and cried. She begged me to go back, but I wouldn't. That was almost five years ago. I hung out on the streets. I stole stuff. I used some drugs. My mom worried herself sick all these years. She'd be waiting for me at the window when I'd come home at one, two in the morning. Sometimes I just stayed out all night. But she'd be there at the window, waiting. I did what I wanted. I didn't care how she felt. I gave her all that grief."

Suddenly, tears were running down the boy's face. "Now she's dead. Maybe I'm the reason why she got sick like she did and died. Maybe she got so sad that it made her sick. It was my fault 'cause I didn't care about her. If I cared about her, she wouldna had to cry so much over the things I did. Maybe Mom died 'cause of me."

"No, that's not why she got sick and died, Cruz," Dorotea consoled him.

"How do you know? You don't know nothin' about it," Cruz growled angrily. "You don't know nothin' about anything!"

"Cruz," Dorotea asserted, "I can tell a lot about people by looking into their eyes. The eyes are the windows to the soul. You have compassion and goodness in your eyes, Cruz. You were wild for a while. But you didn't mean to hurt your mom, and she knew that. That's why she loved you so much. I think right now your mom is in a better place. She's watching over you, Cruz. She's wanting you to remember all the happy times you had with her. She wants you to be happy now too."

They walked a little longer and found a yellow cactus flower. Cruz knelt by the bloom and hung his head. Dorotea knelt next to him and put her hand on his back. Then they both got up slowly and returned to where the other boys were sitting.

The five boys and Dorotea downed the ice cold sodas. Dorotea announced, "I live in the *barrio* too."

"You do?" Cruz asked. "Whereabouts?"

"Adams Avenue," the girl answered.

"My sisters go to school there," Cruz remarked. "We live on Starling."

"I know where that is," Dorotea noted. "Not far from us."

Before they all left for home, Dorotea and the five boys took another long walk in the desert. A jack rabbit bounded away from them. They came across many more wildflowers. Paul told Dorotea about the time a rattlesnake had bitten him here in the desert. Cruz and Beto carried him to where the EMT responders gave him first aid. They had saved his life. Even Cruz smirked a little when Beto teased Paul. "Hey Paul," he called out to him, "I wonder what's underneath this rock? Wanna look?"

Then the sun began its long downward journey. The shadows got longer and longer. The group head back to where they were parked.

"You know, Cruz," Dorotea suggested, "you could call me sometime in the *barrio*. We could, you know, just be friends. I know I'm not all that, but you could call me sometime. We could just sorta hang out. We

165

could get coffee or something. Maybe see a movie. No big deal."

Cruz didn't say anything for long while. Then he answered. "Yeah, that would be okay. Sometimes I'd just like to hang out with somebody, you know. Like you say, no big deal. But I like to go to the movies sometimes. We could do that, yeah."

Cruz looked at the young woman more closely, "You sure you don't have a boyfriend? You're . . . you know, kinda pretty, Dorotea," Cruz commented.

"Thanks," Dorotea replied. "I mean for saying I'm pretty."

She reached into the pocket of her shorts and took out a scrap of paper. She wrote her cell phone number on it. "You can get me here. I'd sure like it if you called, Cruz." Impulsively then, she reached out and gave Cruz a hug. "Hang in there," she whispered.

The boys pulled away in the green van. Dorotea was still standing there, waving. Cruz looked out the side window and waved back.

"She's nice," Cruz remarked. "She's really nice. When I was on the street, I met a lotta chicks. They were okay, but not like her. She was somethin'. I can't believe she was just there with her father like that."

"Stuff like that happens sometimes," Paul commented. He sounded very thoughtful. Ernesto thought that wasn't like him. "It's almost," Paul added, "like it's supposed to happen."

Beto dropped Cruz off first at the apartment on Starling. All four boys gave him hugs before they drove off.

"Cruz seems better," Paul Morales noted. "Did you guys notice that? His darkness sort of lifting . . . just a little. Did you guys see that? I mean, when we started out today, he was really down. He looked like he didn't want to go on. But now . . . "

"What just happened?" Ernesto asked. "I mean, with that girl, Dorotea. Was she for real?"

Paul laughed and looked at Abel.

"Nothin' can lift a guy's spirits like a pretty girl," Abel chuckled. "You know, Cruz's mom is dead, and she was a warm and loving lady. Cruz needed another warm and loving and soft person to help him along. Guys can help guys. But somebody soft like Dorotea, soft like his mom was, she could really reach him. We couldn't."

"You got that right," Paul agreed.

"Let me understand this," Ernesto said. "We go out to the Anza-Borrego Desert. By coincidence, there's a pretty chick camping right there with her pop. She comes over and makes nice with Cruz. It's like the chick appeared out of a sandstorm or something. What's going on, Paul? Am I out of the loop or what?"

Abel grinned at Ernesto. "Sorry, *amigo*. I knew and Beto knew. But you have that big, honest face of yours. We were afraid you'd let the cat out of the bag."

"What cat?" Ernesto asked.

"Well, Ernie," Paul explained. "It's like this. I knew that Cruz needed to have a nice chick. A warm, friendly girl. But what if I'd told him I'd like to introduce him to this sweet chick in the *barrio*—Dorotea. He just wouldn't go for it. But what if we go out to the Anza-Borrego to look for flowers? Then this chick is there, and they start talking. Well, I figured we had a fighting chance that way."

"So it was a setup," Ernesto said.

"Yep," Paul replied. "Dorotea works for me at the computer store. I hired her when that other dude started helpin' himself to cell phones. She's a great girl. Lotta heart. She lives with her dad in the *barrio*. I told her all about this friend of mine. Told her about this guy who was going to pieces over losing his mom. I told Dorotea that this dude means a lot to me. He was drownin', and somebody had to throw him a lifeline. I thought they would click. Dorotea agreed to meet him. So we plotted to be there at that camping spot today. I don't know if anything will come of it. But maybe she and Cruz'll hit it off, at least for a while. You know, he just needs somebody to help him through the worst of this."

"Wow!" Ernesto laughed. "I am awed by you, dude."

"Well, Cruz got the chance to pour out his grief. And he had a sympathetic ear. I knew he was blaming himself for his mom getting sick. I read this psychology book. It said a lot of kids, especially young men, get to thinkin' when they lose their mothers. They think back on the times they weren't the greatest sons in the world. Then they kinda start believin' they caused the mom to die. I knew Cruz was caught up in that."

Paul looked at Ernesto. "Cruz has a long way to go yet. But this helped a lot. I'm thinking in a few days me and Carmen'll go out somewhere. Maybe Cruz and Dorotea can come along too and, you know, keep it going."

"You know, Paul," Ernesto chuckled, "you're something else."

"The question is—*what*?" Paul responded, laughing.

"Carmen has herself a winner," Ernesto declared. "And the girl knows it."

"I don't know about that," Paul objected. "Every time I go to the Ibarra house to pick her up, it's the same thing. Old Emilio is standin' there lookin' at me like the devil just pulled up. His mustache is always twitchin' like crazy. And Lourdes, the older sister, she stands there wringin' her hands like a little old lady."

Paul smirked. "Only one in that house on my side—if you can believe it—is Ivan Redondo. You know, that dorky dude Lourdes is gonna marry. At first I hated the guy, but then we had a long talk. He had a really bad time at his high school, being bullied by everybody. I sympathized with the dude. Now we're buddies . . . "

"I'm with you dude," Ernesto responded, "I remember when I first started going to the Martinez house to pick up Naomi. Poor Mrs. Martinez was hiding out somewhere. Mr. Martinez was giving me dirty looks. The only friend I could rely on was Brutus the dog, as long as I scratched him behind the ears."

When Ernesto got home, his mother was on the phone with her mom in Los Angeles. "No Mom," she was speaking in a patient but weary voice. "Alfredo is not running me ragged. He's a very good baby. . . . What? I do *not* sound cranky Mom. . . . What? Postpartum depression? I never heard of anything so ridiculous. I don't have postpartum depression, Mom. . . . No, absolutely not. I'm deliriously happy. Okay, Mom . . ."

Mom listened to *Abuela* for a while. Grandmother probably gave up trying to convince her daughter she was depressed. "What's going on right now?" Mom asked. "Well, Ernie is out in the desert looking for rattlesnakes with some boys who give me the creeps. Not *all* of them, but a couple of them anyway. . . . What do you mean, Mom? I should forbid my almost seventeen-year-old son to spend a day with his friends? Mom, what century are you living in? What planet do you live on? Oh! Ernie's home. I think. I just heard the door slam. I have to go, Mom. I must start dinner."

Abuela wasn't letting Mom off the hook yet. "The book? Of course not. I haven't forgotten the book. In fact, I was able to finish writing it just before little Alfredo came along. My agent has it right now. She's shopping it around. . . . I think so. . . . Yes, Mom. I need to see Ernie now. I have to find out if a rattlesnake bit him out there today. . . . Yes, I'm joking, Mom. Bye now."

Mom turned to see Ernesto coming into the room.

"Hi Mom. Grandma good as usual?" Ernesto asked.

"Don't be sarcastic," Mom commanded. "We all have our issues, Ernie. Did you see any rattlesnakes?"

"No," Ernesto responded, "just big red flowers. And a beautiful girl was out there too."

"A beautiful girl? What was she doing there?" Mom asked.

"Paul Morales rubbed a lamp," Ernesto explained, "And out came this pretty girl to talk to Cruz and make him feel better."

"Why do I even bother asking you questions?" Mom commented darkly. "Excuse me now, while I spend some quality time with my *good* son."

Ernesto plopped into a living room chair, laughing. Mom's reaction tickled. But Paul's trick in the desert also amused him.

He really admired Paul for what he did today. Paul's girlfriend Carmen once said that no one could have a better friend or a worse enemy than Paul Morales. Today Paul proved what a friend he was to Cruz. Paul would never forget that Cruz had once saved his life when Paul was bitten by that rattlesnake.

As Ernesto relaxed in the chair, Juanita appeared. "She's with *him* again," she declared with a pouty face.

"Yeah," Ernesto said sympathetically. "She yelled at me. She said I was her bad son and Alfredo was her good son."

174

Juanita's eyes widened. "Mama said *that*?" she gasped.

"Not in so many words, but that's what she meant," Ernesto told her. "But don't worry, Juanita. Mom still loves you and Katalina 'cause you're girls. She loves her little girls. I'm the one who has to worry. Alfredo's a boy. He's a boy, and he's taken my place."

Ernesto was just teasing Juanita. He felt especially guilty when she sat on the arm of his chair and put her little arms around his neck. "Don't you worry, Ernie," she told him sincerely. "I love you much more than I love him. He's messy and noisy and stuff."

"This is true, Juanita," Ernesto agreed. He swung Juanita onto his knee and bounced the giggling little girl. "But one day," he told her, "Alfredo won't be so messy and noisy. Then maybe you'll love him more than you love me."

"No," Juanita told him solemnly. "I'll always love you best, Ernie. And you know that. Don't feel bad, Ernie. I think Mama loves you just as much as she loves Alfredo. A mama has to love all her children the same. She can't help it. She just has to."

"Wow!" Ernesto exclaimed. "I'm glad to hear that, Juanita. I was a little worried there. You've made me feel much better. Thank you very much."

Juanita smiled proudly and jumped off Ernesto's knee. She went to find *Abuela*. She wanted to finish the jigsaw puzzle they were working on.

On the following Monday, the relationship between Mira Nuñez and Clay Aguirre was strange. Ernesto noticed that they were together, but they didn't seem close. Mira looked unhappy, and Clay looked grim.

When Mira and Clay were in English class with Kenny Trujillo, the tension was high.

In Ms. Ambler's history class, Ernesto noticed Kenny glancing at Mira a lot. Every time he did, Clay gave him a look of hate.

Ms. Ambler was an older teacher, nearing retirement. She'd been a good teacher in earlier times. Now she was waiting for retirement with more and more eagerness. She found her students harder to control. She longed for how it was thirty-five years earlier, when she began her teaching career.

"President Franklin Roosevelt," she lectured, "dealt with the Great Depression of the 1930s with bold new programs. Can somebody name one of these programs and describe what it did?" Ms. Ambler asked.

"He started the WPA, the Works Progress Administration," Mira Nuñez answered. "That provided a lot of jobs for people in construction. They built schools and bridges. And it even gave jobs to writers and musicians who couldn't find work anywhere else."

"That's right, Mira," Ms. Ambler said. "That is very good. The WPA was a lifeline for a lot of unemployed Americans in those dire times."

Kenny Trujillo raised his hand. "President Roosevelt put in the NYA, the

National Youth Administration. That gave jobs to teenagers and young adults. It helped them stay in school. It was a big help to kids our age in those days."

"Very good, Kenny," Ms. Ambler said to him. She noticed that Clay Aguirre turned in his seat and glared back at Kenny Trujillo. Ms. Ambler was annoyed. Clay was, as usual, not paying attention to what was going on in class. "Clay, can you mention a program of that period that helped struggling Americans?" she asked.

Clay turned and glared at the teacher. He thought she was too old to be teaching. He was getting a C in the class, and he blamed Ms. Ambler. He thought a younger teacher would have kept him interested so he'd be getting better grades. "Uh . . . they tried to stimulate building. They, uh, gave money to people so they could buy new homes and stuff," he answered.

Some of the students laughed. Kenny Trujillo commented, "No, that's something the government did just a little while ago, not back in Roosevelt's time."

"That's right, Kenny," Ms. Ambler agreed. "Clay, you better reread Chapter 34."

Clay looked at Mira. His mistake seemed to amuse her. Clay Aguirre figured she liked that Kenny Trujillo humiliated him. Clay was boiling mad—Mira wasn't going to get away with humiliating him.

CHAPTER TEN

Later in the morning, Ernesto and Naomi were standing by the mural of Cesar Chavez on the science building. Mira Nuñez came along with her backpack bouncing on her shoulders.

"Hi Mira," Naomi called out. "You look fired up."

"You guys," Mira called back and walked up to them. "You know how I was telling you about my mom dating this guy for several months? Then all of a sudden he dumps her? She's all down in the pits and everything? Mom broke down last night and called the jerk. She tried to make up with him. She was like apologizing for whatever it was that made him mad."

"Oh man!" Naomi groaned, "what a bummer!"

"Well, you know what the jerk told her?" Mira went on. "He said he didn't like her as much as he used to. That's why he's been stonewalling her. He said he's kinda into somebody else now. Can you imagine her hanging all that time? He's not even interested in her anymore. He didn't even have the decency to call Mom and let her know."

"She's lucky to be rid of the creep," Naomi told Mira.

"Mom was so sad and weepy," Mira sighed. "I mean, I've had enough! I mean, I love my mom a lot. She's been there for me. She's a great mom. But I talked to her last night like I never did before. It was more like a mom talking to a daughter than the other way around. It felt weird, but Mom needed it."

Mira *was* fired up. "I told my mom that she's an executive in her company. Twenty-two people in the sales department answer to her. She's a great manager, and she earns good money. That glass ceiling that's supposed to keep women from getting to the top, she crashed right through. All she had was sheer talent and guts. I told her, 'Mom, you deserve better than a jerk like this. You don't need this kinda man! You're already a strong, successful woman and the mother of a kid who loves you. You don't need to settle for any old jerk in your life!'"

"Good for you, Mira," Ernesto encouraged her.

"Yeah," Mira affirmed. "Mom's eyes got real big, and she started to cry. She sat there for a few minutes. Then she came over and gave me a big hug. 'I needed that, baby,' she said, 'I really needed that.'"

"Wow!" Naomi exclaimed. "That's great Mira."

"Yeah," Ernesto agreed. "Now maybe you need to take some of your own advice when it comes Clay."

Mira blinked. "Uh, that's sorta different," she replied. "Clay really does care for me. . . ." She started to say more, but then she grew quiet.

"Think about it, girl," Ernesto advised.

Ernesto and Naomi walked toward their next classes. Naomi remarked, "Babe, it's easy to see somebody else making a mistake. It's not so easy to face ourselves making the same mistakes."

"I guess," Ernesto agreed. "I was maybe out of line to say that to Mira. But it makes me so mad the way Aguirre treats her."

"Uh, Ernie, by the way," Naomi changed the subject. "You're gonna be seventeen in two weeks. I know there's gonna be a big party at your house. And a party at Hortencia's. But me and a couple of your really close friends would like to have a little beach party to celebrate. Just our little group. No big thing. Just Abel barbecuing and me and a couple of others."

"I don't want any gifts," Ernesto insisted. "None of my friends have a lot of money. If you want us to go down to the beach and have a little party, that's good."

"Okay then," Naomi confirmed. "Next Sunday afternoon then. Seagull Beach would be good. It'll give our little group time to be together. I mean, you're so incredibly special to us who really know you."

Ernesto smiled and gave Naomi a hug. "You're special to me too, babe. More than I can say."

"Abel will bring the barbecue stuff," Naomi said. "And we'll bring sodas for our little bunch of buddies."

Ernesto walked on alone to his next class. He was amazed at what had happened in the last few months. He had come down from Los Angeles and joined the junior class at Cesar Chavez High School. He didn't know a soul. Then Abel Ruiz befriended him. That broke the ice. Carmen Ibarra came next. Then a few others got to know him. Ernesto felt really touched that his little band of close friends wanted to throw a beach party for him. Of course, Naomi, Carmen, and Abel would be there. Yvette Ozono and Phil Serra would probably come. His friends from the track team might also show up—Julio Avila, Dom Reynosa, and Carlos Negrete. That would probably be about it. That would be a nice, cozy little group. Ernesto once heard a guy say something on the radio: If you made one or two good friends in your life, you were blessed. Ernesto felt really blessed. Ernesto would have maybe seven people at his beach party. Or at least five, if Dom and Carlos didn't come. Five was a good number.

At lunchtime, Ernesto and Julio were walking toward their usual lunch spot. They noticed Clay Aguirre coming the other way, looking for Mira. Clay's hands were gathered into fists, and they swung at his sides. Finally, he spotted Mira coming toward him.

"Hey dummy!" Clay yelled. "Waddya you doing—looking for that creep Trujillo so you can get together for lunch?" Did Clay think that Mira had sneaked off with Kenny Trujillo to have lunch somewhere?

185

Mira stopped in her tracks. "Clay, I was looking for *you*," she said. "You've been missing from our lunch spot and . . . "

"You know why, don't you?" Clay snarled. "You been flirting with Trujillo, that's why. Today in history, remember? I made a little mistake about the Depression and Trujillo corrected me. You looked real happy about that."

Naomi and Yvette were coming from their classes, ready to have lunch. They stopped next to Ernesto and Julio. Tessie Zamora joined them. Dom Reynosa and Carlos Negrete walked up to them next. A few other juniors stopped too, drawn by Clay's loud voice.

They all stared silently at Clay and Mira. Then Dom remarked, "Listen to that idiot putting the girl down."

"I wasn't happy about you making a mistake, Clay," Mira whimpered.

"Yes you were," Clay insisted. "You were grinning like a fool. All I've done for you, Mira, and you don't even show me any loyalty. Well, come on, we might as well eat lunch. Get over here! Don't just stand there like an idiot!"

Mira didn't move. A voice went through her mind. It was a voice from earlier in the day. The first time she heard the voice, she had resented it. She didn't think it had anything to do with her. Now, suddenly, she heard the voice again. It pierced her very soul.

"Now maybe you need to take some of your own advice when it comes Clay," Ernesto had told her. She looked directly at Clay.

"I'm getting sick of the way you treat me, Clay," Mira Nuñez declared. "I'm sick and tired of you calling me bad names and treating me like dirt. I haven't done anything wrong. I deserve better, Clay. I'm not taking it anymore. We're done. You've insulted me and humiliated me for the last time."

Clay Aguirre couldn't have looked more shocked if a UFO had landed.

Naomi Martinez clapped, followed by Ernesto, Julio, Dom, and Carlos. They and the other juniors applauded and cheered. Tessie and Carmen were yelling, "Way to go, girl! You rock!" Pretty soon, about two dozen juniors were standing there, cheering and clapping. Clay looked at them all with fury. He was fuming but outnumbered. Clay turned on his heel and fled.

Naomi and Carmen rushed to Mira. "Let's do lunch, girl," Naomi suggested. "I brought fresh cookies, and I'm sharing!" Carmen and Naomi both threw their arms around Mira.

After school that afternoon, Ernesto sat in his living room with Alfredo in his arms. Ernesto was very proud of himself. He had changed the baby twice. Now Alfredo was cooing happily. Ernesto thought his little brother was smiling at him in a brotherly way.

"He likes me, Dad," Ernesto declared. "The brother's bond is right there. I can tell. Look at that grin on his face."

Luis Sandoval laughed. "I think you're right, Ernie. He looks a lot like you did at that age too. All that hair. Those big, warm, brown puppy eyes." Dad didn't tell Ernesto that a newborn baby doesn't know how to smile.

"Mom," Ernesto complained, "Dad just said I have puppy eyes! You mean I look like a dog?"

Maria Sandoval laughed too. "No, you don't look like a dog. But you *do* have puppy eyes. That's one reason everybody loves you so much. A lot of boys have these narrow, shifty eyes. But you've got those big wide gingersnap eyes. People can't help loving you, Ernie."

"Speaking of people who love me," Ernesto said. "A couple—maybe four or five—of my real close friends want to have small party at Seagull Beach to celebrate my birthday. It'll be next Sunday afternoon. I know you guys are planning a party. And there's that thing at Hortencia's. Actually, I don't like so much hoopla. But Abel and

189

Naomi and a few friends want this little beach party."

"That's nice," Mom commented. "In a big party, your friends can't even talk to you. An intimate little beach party for your closest friends, that's a good idea."

"Yeah," Ernesto continued. "I told them no gifts and stuff. Just a little barbecue."

Ernesto rocked Alfredo back and forth very gently. To Ernesto, the baby looked surprised, then happy. He was sure Alfredo was smiling at him.

The brand new life in his arms made Ernesto think about his own life so far. In a few weeks, Ernesto would be seventeen. Ernesto was anxious to be a senior and then to get to college. He wanted to start making things happen in his life and in the world. The adult world beckoned. He felt as though he stood at the water's edge. A great and inviting sea lay before him. It was unseeable, but exciting and wondrous. He was glad that Naomi felt the same way, now that she'd decided to be a medical researcher.

Ernesto reflected on what he wanted to do. He thought he'd go to law school. Then he'd spend some time working at one of those free legal clinics for the poor. His Uncle Arturo Sandoval was a lawyer. He did a lot of work, free of charge, for people in need. Uncle Arturo was a great role model for Ernesto.

Next, when he was established in his law career, Ernesto thought he might run for the state senate or House of Representatives. Maybe none of that would happen. But right now, with his little brother in his lap, it was a wonderful dream.

On Sunday afternoon, Ernesto picked up Naomi at one o'clock. Abel said the little gang of friends would be there around two. Abel, of course, would get there earlier to get the food started. He promised grilled beef.

Ernesto and Naomi had gone to Seagull Beach several times since they had been dating. It was a nice beach with lots of room and fire rings. According to the weather report, the sky would be overcast on Sunday, but the day would be warm. Ernesto thought that would discourage other beachgoers. They'd have Seagull Beach to themselves.

"This is gonna be nice," Ernesto declared as they drove toward the beach. "Just a few close friends."

"Just those who really, *really* love you, Ernie," Naomi affirmed.

"Well, I've tried to be a good friend," Ernesto said.

"Yeah," Naomi agreed, "and you've succeeded, dude."

They parked the Volvo in a spot overlooking the sandy beach. Ernesto took Naomi's hand, leading her down the narrow trail to Seagull Beach. The aroma of the barbecuing beef reached them, and Ernesto smiled. He didn't know of anything in the world as good as the smell of barbecued beef. They spotted Abel down there right away. But then Ernesto was a little disappointed. In spite of the cloud cover, they didn't have Seagull Beach to themselves after all. About a dozen people were down there already.

Ernesto blinked. "Hey," he remarked, "isn't that Dom Reynosa? I didn't recognize him in that hat."

"Yeah," Naomi answered, "he came with Carlos."

"Julio Avila came," Ernesto pointed. "Look. He's unloading the sodas."

Ernesto was also saw Yvette Ozono and her boyfriend, Phil Serra, just arriving. But Jorge Aguilar and Eddie Gonzales from the track team were a surprise.

And it sounded like more cars were arriving up on the highway.

Carmen and Paul Morales were coming down the trail, followed by Beto Ortiz. Cruz Lopez was coming too, with that girl he met in the desert—Dorotea. Cruz was holding her hand on the trail, just as Ernesto had held Naomi's hand. Tessie Zamora and Mira Nuñez came then. Abel's girlfriend, Claudia Villa, was carrying the buns. She started putting them out as soon as she got to the beach.

Ernesto stared at them all, dumb-founded.

Lourdes Ibarra, Carmen's sister, came with her boyfriend, Ivan Redondo. Then other kids showed up. Ernesto hardly knew them. They were the ones he tutored from time to time, when they were struggling in one class or another. There was a girl whose name Ernesto didn't even know. One day a guy had made an insulting remark about her weight. She was crying, and Ernesto talked to her. He told her she had the most beautiful smile he ever saw.

There were more than twenty people now, then twenty-five. They all arranged themselves around the fire rings. Abel and Claudia gave out roast beef sandwiches with all the fixings. By the time they had all finished eating and were drinking their sodas, about thirty of Ernesto Sandoval's closest friends were partying on Seagull Beach.

Paul Morales stood up. "Dude," he began, looking at Ernesto, "you said you didn't want any gifts. Okay. We decided to do somethin' different. You might be wonderin' why so many of us showed up. Well, we couldn't afford gifts. You were right about that. But we can tell you how much you've meant to us. Thanks, *amigo*, for your friendship. Thanks for reaching out to a rough-edged dude like me with a rattlesnake tattooed on his hand." Paul flashed that grin of his. "Thanks for not judging me. Thanks for unconditional friendship, even when it was hard to give. Happy birthday, Ernie!"

Cruz Lopez got up. "Thanks, man, for helping me and my family. It meant more than I can say."

"Thanks, Ernie," Yvette added, "for reaching out to me when I gave up. Thanks for being there at Tommy Alvarado's funeral. Thanks for letting me know I wasn't alone. Thanks for making me feel special through it all."

"Thanks for cheering for me on the track meet when I beat your pants off," Julio told Ernesto.

One by one, boys and girls, they told Ernesto why he was special to them. Some of them he scarcely knew, except for one act of kindness he had almost forgotten. But they remembered.

The last to speak was the overweight girl. "Thanks Ernie. You were the only boy who ever told me I was cute and that I had a beautiful smile. That warmed my heart for weeks. I clung to your words like a drowning person clings to a life raft. Happy birthday, Ernie."

Naomi walked over to Ernie and put her arms around him. "And thank you, Ernie, for loving me. Your love is the greatest gift I ever got."

Everybody applauded. Ernesto looked out at the faces. He was a big, tall, almost seventeen-year-old young man. With his running and lifting weights, he was pretty muscular. With his mop of dark hair blowing in the wind, he looked like a *macho* Latino guy. In spite of all that, tears welled in his eyes, and he wasn't ashamed when they ran down his face. His heart was so full of gratitude for Naomi and all his friends. He couldn't help himself.

He glanced at the surf, only yards away. He was at the water's edge of that large, inviting sea that he had seen the other night with Alfredo in his lap. Before long, he would launch himself on that sea. Before long, he would set out to make his dreams come true.

For now, however, he told himself he'd made a good start. Right here, in the *barrio*. Right here, with all his friends.